A SETTLEMENT
OF MEMORY

Also by Gordon Rodgers

Poetry

Floating Houses — 1984
The Pyrate Latitudes — 1986

Fiction

The Phoenix: A Novella — 1985

A SETTLEMENT OF MEMORY

A Novel

by

GORDON RODGERS

killick press
an imprint of Creative Publishers
St. John's, Newfoundland
1999

THE CANADA COUNCIL | LE CONSEIL DES ARTS
FOR THE ARTS | DU CANADA
SINCE 1957 | DEPUIS 1957

We acknowledge the support of The Canada Council for the Arts for our
publishing program.

We acknowledge the financial support of the Department for Canadian
Heritage for our publishing program.

Author's Note

*A Settlement of Memory is a work of fiction. Though I have borrowed from
Newfoundland's history, geography, and political record, the story told has been bound by none of them; no
person, place or event described herein has reality or reference beyond the fiction.*

∞ Printed on acid-free paper

Published by
KILLICK PRESS
an imprint of CREATIVE BOOK PUBLISHING
a division of 10366 Newfoundland Limited
a Robinson-Blackmore Printing & Publishing associated company
P.O. Box 8660, St. John's, Newfoundland A1B 3T7

FIRST EDITION
Typeset in 12 point Centaur

Printed in Canada by:
ROBINSON-BLACKMORE PRINTING & PUBLISHING

Canadian Cataloguing in Publication Data

Rodgers, Gordon
    A settlement of memory

    ISBN 1-894294-05-X

I. Title

PS8585.03903S4   1999   C813'.54   C99-950103-8
PR9199.3.R423S4   1999

For Christopher, David and Paula

and

IN MEMORIAM

Percy Janes

Two things only are wicked:
to be helpless when you could be free,
to be hungry when you could be fed.
— Gwyn Thomas

. . . the struggle of man against power is
the struggle of memory against forgetting.
— Milan Kundera

. . . the act of writing becomes a settlement of memory . . .
— Terrence Des Pres

*I*n a dark and inaccessible corner of the studio none of the pictures have been framed. A few pinned to the wall have curled into cylinders, but most gather dust on the floor in an untidy discard pile.

These pictures reveal the men and women that have lately peopled the wild rumours about Tom Vincent. From these pictures Tom himself gazes out, euphorically intoxicated and smiling, or in sozzled consternation, frowning. His tie, if not missing altogether, is always loose, his white collar unbuttoned. In several he is in shirt-sleeves. Giddy good-timers crowd into the pictures with him.

To this corner, Ray Pike turned on a whisky whim, raising his glass to all in solidarity. He downed the last of the drink just as Tom entered the studio. He was wearing a very fine, very expensive charcoal-gray suit. In his hand he carried a matching fedora which he dropped on the table. Without a word he took his seat in front of the camera. George Gill followed him in, leaned back against the wall to wait and watch. He noticed the empty bottle.

Pike went to work. He looked into his camera, then up, concerned.

"It's not right," he said. "I don't know what's wrong, but it's not right."

He repositioned the camera, once, then again, but still it did not suit him.

"What in hell's flames are you doing, Ray?" Tom asked, but he did not wait for an answer. He stood, walked to the table, and took his hat in hand.

"I know when it's no good," the photographer said softly.

George nodded to the bottle. "Perhaps a little too much too early to do your best work, Ray?" George looked at Tom, and Tom looked straight back at him. "It happens sometimes," he continued, "to the best of us."

Tom put his hat on.

"That's it," Pike said.

Tom and George stopped glaring at each other to glare at Pike.

"What's what?" Tom asked.

"The hat. Leave the hat on." He motioned Tom back to the chair. "Sit. Sit."

Tom hesitated.

"*C'mon, Tom, do it!*" Pike ordered.

"Right away, *sir!*" Tom's eyes were wide in mock surprise. He scuttled back to the chair with such exaggerated and obedient haste that Pike and George laughed out loud.

The photographer pointed to the lens. "Now look here," he said. Tom did as he was told, but glanced at George again. Pike saw that, but released the shutter anyway.

The white flash blinded Tom for a moment, and in his moment of blindness he saw:

> God's finger hook glowing tobacco
> from Tim O'Brien's pipe into the hay
> spark and start the Great Fire;
>
> the switch thrown in Union Cove:
> light in the dark;
>
> and, inexplicable,
> blooming flowers of fire
> punching the night;
> the tiniest of flashes,
> a lick of fire.

Of all the pictures taken of Tom Vincent, it is this black-and-white photograph that comes to mind whenever his name is spoken:

His head is thrown back in a haughty pose, but whatever is prideful or arrogant in his attitude is neutralized by the echo of a smile.

Beneath the hat, loose black hair coils out, and the eyes, brown in life, are black and constant. The focus of his vision is somewhere outside the picture's frame of reference. He sees what no one else sees, and that trace of a smile mocks you just a little for not seeing.

He is clean-shaven. His cheeks are pitted and pockmarked by the skin condition of his adolescence, and those scars suggest a hard maturity born of difficult times.

He has broad strong shoulders, and the hard labour necessary to bring the shoulders to that shape seems out of keeping with such a fine tailored suit with matching hat.

It was Tom's favourite photograph of himself. When he first saw it, he had twenty thousand copies printed as postcards and sent one to every member of the Fishermen's Collective.

PART I

I Tom Vincent, only child of Colin and Angela Vincent, was born on a November night in 1876 on the south side of St. John's.

Years later, on the deck of the ocean liner *CLIO*, Tom would tell Hammond Janes that the birth provoked no strange or wondrous occurrences in the heavens. Hammond noted a wistfulness in Tom's voice as he spoke, as if he wished it had been otherwise.

What Tom told of his earliest years had more of sense and summary than scene. Because those recollections dovetailed almost too neatly with the later course of his life, Hammond suspected Tom of both cutting and colouring his memories.

Tom was brought into the world that November night by a midwife in an upstairs bedroom of a house his father had bought cheaply some years before and restored. That, in its own way, was wonder enough: through hard work his father had fashioned a good and solid house and owed money to no one when the work was done. This in times when it was the most common fate to be indebted to the very last of your days. But Colin Vincent had a passion to be beholden to no one.

He taught Tom that the man you owe money to owns you.

Colin hailed from the North Shore of Bonavista Bay. In middle age after short deliberation and long labour he managed (just) to pay off what he always seemed to be owing at the store, then he moved to St. John's. He went to work for regular pay as a foundryman with the Lank Company. Thus he freed himself for all time from the Bay and the uncertain fishery. As far as Colin Vincent was concerned, his was a model to be followed.

So, from earliest days, Tom knew men could change their lives.

The Lank Company on Water Street specialized in and prided itself on its production of nails and spikes — "all sizes, for all needs" — and, the foundrymen added, "from crib to crucifixion" and then they allowed under breath that they were the ones being crucified.

The factory occupied a blackened three-story brick block of a building. Broad chimneys boiled black smoke out everywhere and not a single pane of glass was ungrimed. Likewise inside. It was a dirty place to work. The glowing molten metal was an intense thing unto itself and it carried to the nostrils, as its sign, acrid smells that burned in the nose. The air rang with sharp metallic clatter, and short aggressive hisses issued from dark corners while confused orders were shouted half-heard and half-heeded from high above the floor, from across the floor, from everywhere at once.

Once on a Sunday afternoon when Tom was very young his father took him to visit the place. Just inside the gate Tom stepped on a nail that pierced boot leather and foot flesh and that brought the outing to a screeching, tearful end.

The foundry workers regularly sustained puncture wounds. They thought nothing of those, but none could ignore burns from spattering molten metal. Even the smallest droplet bore pain enough to weaken the strongest men and burns always scarred. In parts of the foundry where Colin did not usually work, he often saw men who'd taken falls that drove splintered bones sharp and bloody through muscle and skin, so he did not complain about the minor rips and searings he suffered and which Angela most capably dressed.

Angela was from St. John's and a contrast in all ways to her husband. He was as tall, broad and dark as she was small and pale. If he was a rough and inarticulate force, then she was an atmosphere — pale, soft-spoken, clear both in word and action. With the young Tom as her reluctant companion she attended at least one church service every Sunday. She reminded him always of his Christian duty to remember his God in the days of his youth.

As far back as he could remember he had helped his mother dress his father's wounds. She said he had a gift for it, but what she saw in him or how she knew this, he did not know. Mostly he watched her work. He was never squeamish, though his mother sometimes was, and in moments when she doubted what next to do, she would turn to Tom. Eyes focused on the wound, he would look up and shake his head and she would cease her ministrations, or he would nod, and she would continue whatever she was doing, wrapping with a cloth bandage perhaps.

She often scolded Colin for not cleaning his wounds at work. No time, Colin would protest, then he'd tell her about horrendous dry heat burns or impacted fractures that others had suffered and yet worked on, and if they had worked on, how could he not?

Over this, and many other things, Tom could remember Colin and Angela in friendly conflict. Their differences stemmed, he would later come to realize, from the fact that his mother, born and bred in St. John's, was a 'townie', and his father an outharbour bayman. Though Angela would never deny Colin's virtues, hard work and loyalty foremost amongst them, she tried always to improve his speech and to teach him the manners that would make him more acceptable to friends and acquaintances, and, especially, to her sisters. While she tried to teach him manners, he tried to help her understand the real powers of the world — the clergy, the merchant-men and the politicians — that the common folk were up against.

She spoke in a smooth Irish brogue, he in a rough Dorset burr.

As Tom grew older he learned to speak in both their tongues. Thus his parents unwittingly bestowed on him a gift for words and an ear for sounds that would eventually enable him to transpose his speeches into any dialect he heard.

In the same upstairs bed where Tom had been born twelve years before, Angela lay dying. Her many sisters descended on the house like a flock of meddlesome angels. They hurried about doing all that needed to be done, and they fussed over Tom and his father, but out of concern for Tom they denied him what he most of all desired, free access to his mother.

He overheard the sisters as they reasoned it out among themselves: He is only a child — it will be too much for him. She is too sick — it will be too much for her. Better for both mother and son that visits be few and short, and conversation controlled. The first time they allowed him to visit, Aunt Rebecca, the oldest sister, sat stiffly in a chair on the far side of the bed, a stern-looking overseer.

Never before had his mother looked so pale, or so small. She was a seamstress whose work brought small but sorely needed sums of money into the household. When she sewed, Tom often thought her hands and fingers moved as if possessed of a nimble knowledge all their own. But now they lay so flat and pale on the smoothed and straightened blankets, he did not expect them to move at all. But his mother opened her eyes, smiled and reached out for his hand. Her grip was as strong as ever. He bent to kiss her, but she shook her head.

"Best not," she whispered in a low rasping voice. "Just in case." The paleness, he'd been told, was a common symptom of a respiratory problem which few were able to overcome. Every breath his mother took was insufficient, and taken with effort.

"We must not speak too much, Angela," Aunt Rebecca said.

"Are you fine, Mom?"

Aunt Rebecca answered, "About the same."

Angela gave a little smile, nodded, whispered, "You?"

"Sure the boy's fine, Angela," Aunt Rebecca said. "Don't trouble yourself about that. What could be wrong with him at his young age?"

His mother gave his hand a reassuring squeeze. Then turning her head a little towards him so her sister could not see, she gave him a slow, deliberate wink. Then she smiled, and her smile set all things right with him.

Too soon, he had to leave. Even worse, because of the strong family resemblance, he could not look at any of the sisters, who seemed to be everywhere about the house, without seeing his mother.

He was permitted one visit per day, but never on his own. Angela contented herself with holding his hand tightly, looking into his eyes and smiling. In this way, though he soon noticed her grip weakening from day to day, she communicated a sense of fearless calm to him. Helplessly, he looked back at her, and wished he could do more.

She unexpectedly let go of his hand one day. With motions of hand and eye executed as expertly as a sewing manoeuvre, she bid him to bring his head down close to hers. Her hand, just as gentle and fluid as it could be, found the back of his head and pulled him closer still. "For sure and certain," she whispered into his ear, "you will do well in this life." She pressed a kiss hard on his cheek. "Go now," she said, her hand finding his chest and gently, weakly, pushing him away. As he straightened up, she smiled. She closed her eyes, and her hand fell to the bed as if no strength at all were left in it. Before Aunt Rebecca could comment on what was happening, it was over.

Next day his visit was brief. She did not open her eyes or speak. Her breathing was short and shallow, her forehead beaded with sweat.

Then, for a few days, he was not allowed to visit at all.

Then they told him she was gone.

Could he have been stronger in standing up to the sisters? Given the chance, he asked himself, was there something more he could have done? Something he should have said?

As soon as the funeral was over, Tom's father went back to the foundry. Though Colin seldom spoke of Angela, Tom likened his father's grief to an oversized greatcoat that he always wore. Tom tried to be as stoic as his father. It might even be said his grief was less in evidence, outwardly, than that of his father. Inwardly, though, the depth of Tom's loss was matched only by the persistence of self-doubt. Somehow, the one sustained the other.

He decided to quit school to go to work to make up for his mother's lost income. As a protest against her death, he quit the church at the same time.

For the first few months there was a gulf of silence between father and son. It worried Tom. Every morning, before dawn, he heard his father drag himself out of bed. His father did not wash, did not prepare anything to eat. He might or might not look in on Tom. Only a few minutes after waking, he would be leaving the house. In the dark silent time between his father's leaving and his getting up himself to look for work, Tom imagined the worst for his father, and for himself. Though his father had never more than slapped him on the arse a time or two in twelve years, Tom worried his father might now start to beat him. Likewise he worried that his father might do something to harm himself, though his father had never, by any word or action, indicated any such intention. Given a choice between his two unfounded fears, Tom would choose the former. He had no mother. He needed his father, and would live with him regardless.

When Tom wasn't out looking for work he busied himself around the house. He split wood, hauled water, cooked meals, found and sealed a clever leak in the porch roof. He waited and hoped, in vain, for some sign of approval from his father. Until, one day, as Tom was splitting wood he caught his father watching him from the kitchen window, an amused expression on his face. He came out to the chopping block then, put his hand on his son's shoulder, and nodded.

Looking at the bright mound of split wood and nodding his head he said, "Good, Tom, good." Then after a moment, "More than enough here to last the winter. Slow down a bit. Pace yourself."

Tom sensed his father gradually getting back to himself. And once Colin was certain that Tom was serious about not going back to school, he found a job for him in no time at all as a general labourer on the Baird Premises. The Bairds were merchandisers with special interests in shipping and the fishery. Tom was tall for his years and still growing, but, because of his age, they only paid him half-a-man wages.

Six days of the week for two years, Tom and his father left for work together, usually before dawn. Both enjoyed the cool silence, the dark solitude, of the early morning walk. In winter the only sound as they set out was the crunching of the snow beneath their feet. The rest of the year, it was the crunch of gravel. In summer they often caught first light beaming through the Narrows, brightening houses and all, and flashing off the windows. These were the best mornings. They more than made up for wet mornings of rain, drizzle and fog, and for the cold and snow of wintry weather. They walked along the southside path and then across the old wooden bridge to Water

Street. Here, for the first time, they would meet others, like themselves, on their way to work. Sometimes someone might wave, but most were content to walk on in silence, to leave everyone to their thoughts. Tom and his father seldom spoke before reaching the Baird Premises.

"Give them a good day's work, Tom," his father would say before walking on to the foundry. "I told them you would."

Workdays were long and hard. In winter it was dark hours before they arrived home. They were both ready for sleep after cleaning up supper dishes. Colin would sit at the kitchen table for a draw on his pipe. Tom would lie on the daybed, and many nights he was fast asleep. His father lifted him in his arms to carry him upstairs, but Tom always woke up, and insisted he could walk up on his own, and then, eyes closed, he would half-stumble up the stairs and flop into bed.

Tom tried to stay awake because his father, as he never had before, took to passing the evenings telling stories about the life he'd led before he'd come to St. John's, before meeting Angela. He told Tom how it was during the years he'd spent as a fisherman, about the adventures he'd had on the ice, and the things he'd seen as a schoonerman on the high seas. Tom tried to stay awake, but often could not. In the morning his father's stories were half-remembrance and half-dream, or some such mixture of the two. His father never spoke about the foundry, where he seemed to be having a run of good luck with regard to injury. He always wanted to know how Tom was doing at Baird's.

After supper one winter evening about a year after Angela had died, Tom was lying on the daybed, feeling warm and tired. The lanterns had been turned down low. His father was sitting on one of the kitchen chairs, his stockinged feet resting and warming on the open oven door of the stove. He held his pipe in one hand, puffing away. He turned to Tom and said, quietly, "You've done so well, son, your mother would be as proud of you as I am." He smiled sheepishly. "She'd be pleased with me, too, I think." His eyes glistened in the lantern light. "We're going to be all right," he said.

Tom nodded. His father nodded back, took out his handkerchief and blew his nose, and that was when Tom knew his father had finally cut the greatcoat of his grief down to size.

Tom's duties with the Bairds were various. At first he mainly helped load and unload the schooners. This work broadened and strengthened his shoulders, thickened the muscles in his legs. Then someone found out he could read and write and do sums, so he was charged with counting the butts and tubs, barrels and boxes, cases and puncheons, of sugar and butter, pork and beef, biscuits and oranges and molasses that the boats brought in. Sometimes Tom made out Bills of Lading, invoices and receipts, other times he stocked shelves, wrote products and prices on windows with whitewash, swept and mopped floors. He made a point of remembering where just about everything was stored, how much it cost to buy and what it sold for. In time the Bairds trusted him to handle cash.

Of the dozen or so boys working at Baird's, Tom was the tallest and probably the strongest. His reading, writing and arithmetic also singled him out from his fellows, and soon, unofficially, he was their advocate. If the boys had a gripe about work, it was Tom they relied on to speak it plainly to the Bairds. This worked so well for everybody that, after a time, the Bairds made him First Boy. It was easier to deal with a representative of the boys than to deal with each boy individually. No such post had existed before. For Tom it meant a two-percent increase in pay.

Tom enjoyed the freedom from school. It was not so much that he disliked school as that he loved books. There were times during the day when he could safely read in the warehouse. He'd made a place for himself near the largest window, and there, in the best light, he had a chair. The sill was always lined with his books. Here he could read undisturbed. He read whatever he wanted, whatever came in on ships — books of strange adventure, from far-distant countries, by authors unknown in the New World. He read books on weather, books on stars, a complete sea-set of Sir Walter Scott, a compilation of the greatest volcanic eruptions of all time. He read British and American poets who published their thin volumes in

France. These were odd little productions. The poetry Tom knew and remembered best from school was written in four-line stanzas, with a rhyme scheme, and he'd been taught how to scan such poems. The poems in these cheap little books, however, had no rhyme at all, and hardly any lines of uniform length. He kept them, though, as literary curiosities. He found German and Spanish philosophy daunting, even in translation. Pamphlets, religious or secular, he could consume by the bundle. He read two different translations of the *Oneirocriticia* by Artemidorus — the second translation so unlike the first, it was like reading a new book. Sometimes he felt as if he were reading round and round a great mystery. He thought of it as a globe, a smooth sphere crackling with a long-chained lightning of ideas.

After two years with the Bairds, Tom was just under six feet tall.

One day he was called from storeroom to office.

A slender man was waiting for him there. He had a head of white hair and thick grizzled eyebrows joined to form an angry V at the bridge of his nose. He was wearing a dark blue suit and in his hands he held gloves, a shining cane — silver-handled, silver-tipped — and a hat.

"My name is Edward Lank," he said as Tom closed the door. "Your father worked for me. I am, sad to say, here with bad news."

"Bad news?"

Lank nodded. "An accident. Your father had an accident."

"Accident? What kind of accident?"

"Perhaps you should sit," Lank said, motioning to an armchair.

Tom sat. His heart thumped against the wall of his chest, pulsed in his ears. The chair suddenly seemed of unreal depth and softness. "Where is he now? How is he?"

Lank bowed his head for a moment, then looked up at Tom. "There was nothing anyone could do for him. I'm sorry, Tom."

"Why? What do you mean? He's had accidents before."

Lank shook his head. "Not like this."

"What do you mean?"

Colin had fallen from a railless catwalk. A lucky man would've struggled away with broken bones. But a discarded spike in a garbage heap had struck into the base of Colin's skull. He died justlikethat, the doctor said.

For a long while after that Colin lay on the floor of Tom's imagination, Tom believing that if he'd reached his father before they moved him, he could've done something to help, something to save him.

Once again his mother's sisters descended on the house. To everyone's surprise, Edward Lank made a brief visit to pay his respects. He offered condolences to one and all, but especially to Tom, and, as he was leaving, handed Tom a note, handwritten in a fine style on thick, expensive paper. It praised Colin Vincent as one-of-a-kind: a hard worker, dependable and loyal, who would be sorely missed on the foundry floor. Edward Lank paid for the funeral.

Though the funerals were separated by two years, it was almost as if Tom had buried both parents at the same time, as if there had been one funeral. The same ministers presided, the same tear-stained faces sat in the pews, the same crying and wailing rose up behind him. Through it all he tried to absent himself by looking only at the edges of things, by studying shoes, by doing complicated calculations in his head, and the effort brought on a tremendous headache.

Three days after Colin was laid down next to Angela, Edward Lank paid a second visit. Tom let him into the kitchen, then retired to the table where he'd been sitting in a shock of silence. Lank looked at Tom. Since the funeral Tom's cheeks and forehead had broken out in pustules, large and red on his cheeks, small and hard on his forehead. Lank set his hat on the tabletop, carefully laid his cane next to it, took his gloves off finger by finger, placed them across his cane.

"You're young and you'll get over this," he said. "Your life will go on. Take my word for it." Then he sat across the table from Tom. He leaned forward, elbows on the table, crossed his arms. "The question, Master Tom Vincent, is 'What kind of life?' Have you thought about that?"

Tom, blank.

"Hear me out then." Lank uncrossed his arms and leaned back in the chair. "Ben Baird tells me that for a lad of only fourteen, you're a good reliable worker, and strong, too, and a good head on your shoulders, a smart fellow. He's shown me how you've organized your parts of the store, how you keep track of it all and keep your own accounts. What he's telling me about you reminds me of your father. A good man, a hard worker, no complaints. I feel a responsibility to you because of your father," he continued softly, "but your father's gone now and I feel his loss with you." After a long moment during which the softness disappeared from his voice, he continued. "Ben would hate to see you go, but understands that you might want to better yourself now. Despite what's happened, he can still only pay you a little bit better than half-a-man wages. You'll never make it on that now, not without your father's money. No you will not. Tom," he continued, leaning forward again, eyebrows now wedged in deep seriousness, "if you want, you can have your father's job. I'll even pay you his wages. But," he hurried on before Tom could answer, "I've got something else you might want to think about."

He had a small store on Reach Run Island, a tiny island. North. Quite simply, honestly, he couldn't find anyone to work there. "And when I do," he said, "it's hard to keep them up there."

Pointing to Tom, "There's a future there for the right person. Someone young with no ties back here, a good strong worker with a good head on his shoulders. I believe you're the one, Tom Vincent, the very *man* for that job!"

Tom nodded.

"If you decide to go, I can make all the proper arrangements with — "

"I'll go," Tom said, knowing suddenly a desire to be away from all things familiar.

When he opened the door to Lank's store on Reach Run Island, everything he needed had been laid out for him. Shelves were fully stocked, thoughtfully organized. The accounting books were neatly stacked on the counter.

Tom knew those books, long and heavy and bound in black leather, would probably tell a tale. He was leafing through one of them when two fishermen came in and sized him up. When Tom introduced himself as the new storekeeper, they said nothing at first, then asked him to show them how he made out his bills. Tom pulled a receipt book out from beneath the counter, and, as the fishermen watched him carefully, he slowly made up a bill to show them he could both read and write and do additions and subtractions as well.

When he finished, the two fishermen looked at each other, raised their eyebrows, nodded their approval, first to each other, and then to Tom.

"Well," one of them said as they left, "you'll be busy enough."

"You'll do," said the other.

Tom lived quite comfortably in two rooms at the back of the store and he chose to spend most of his time there when he was not working.

The store was well-patronized, partly because there was no other on the island, and partly because almost all the fishermen thereabouts had longstanding accounts. As predicted, he was busy enough keeping their accounts up-to-date, but there was little else he had to do. He never even had to place an order for anything. On a regular basis everything the store sold was shipped to him. Along with the crates and boxes and barrels of hardware and foodstuffs, which Tom helped to unload from the schooner, there also came a fish buyer who delivered a fat envelope in which every item, its cash price, and its times three credit value were listed.

When the schooner was empty, Lank's man graded and bought and filled the holds with whatever amount of fish he wished to buy from the fishermen of Reach Run Island. And, last thing before departure, Lank's agent would inform Tom by what amount each fisherman's indebtedness to Lank should be diminished.

Tom would remember the year he worked there, especially the early months, as a spell of counting and calculation. A dry time. He kept his father out of head and heart by obsessively manipulating numbers, the numbers crowding out all weeping thoughts of his father, and other things, too. He concerned himself with little outside the store.

Tom studied Lank's accounts and soon concluded that things had not changed at all in the years since his father had fished for a living. Lank's store on Reach Run Island functioned in much the same way as the stores his father had described in Bonavista Bay. In all transactions between fisherman and merchantman, there was seldom an exchange of cash, and it was always a case of fishermen's need against merchantmen's greed. The fisherman caught and sold fish to the merchantman at prices arbitrarily set by the merchantman, and the merchantman extended the fisherman enough credit to buy food and clothes and equipment to get through another season. Thus the fishermen survived and the merchantmen thrived, year after year. But what stung the fishermen most of all was knowing that what was bought for a dollar in cash cost three dollars if taken on credit.

Each part of the coast, Tom's father had explained to him, had its own store, so when it came to the buying or selling of fish (and almost anything else for that matter), there was no choice for the fishermen, and no competition for the merchantmen.

Tom's study of the accounts began as an exercise with numbers to keep his mind from dwelling on his father. But soon he found himself thinking about his father more than ever. As Tom better understood how difficult it would be for a fisherman, through sheer hard work, to rise up through the red ink into the black, the greater grew his appreciation for his father's accomplishment, his having done just that, when most could not. The nobler his father grew in his eyes, the more uneasy and ashamed Tom began to feel for working with a merchant.

Besides, storekeeping was dreadfully unchallenging work. Secretly, he hoped to find a way out.

Fortunately he knew many of the schoonermen from St. John's that were working the coast. They liked his way and knew his story so they helped him out whenever they could. They bought small quantities of ship's provisions from him, delivered small packages to the store to save him a walk to the wharf, but mainly they brought him books, books, and more books, through which he escaped from everything.

In one of those books he read of the English experiments with cooperative societies. What spoke to him more than anything else, what he would carry through the years, a diamond in his mind when all the particulars of common ownership, collective effort and equal division of profits were long forgotten: that children in cooperative societies were raised, not only by biological parents but by all cooperative members, every child the responsibility of every adult. He imagined how things would've been different for him if he'd been living in such a world when his mother and father had died. He would not have been left to fend for himself, he would not have been left alone. Home, he imagined, would have been any house he chose to enter.

These imaginings signalled a reawakening of emotions. He began to resent the work he was doing for Edward Lank because it was Lank he was gradually coming to blame for the death of his father on the foundry floor.

On Reach Run Island, the pimples, lumps and bumps that had begun to appear on Tom's face back in St. John's had multiplied. His face was now infused, inflamed and infected. Some vile matter always oozed in some quarter, some spot was always tender, while other places would instantly discharge yellow pus if touched at all.

Even so, after a time, there were a number of young people who came around to see him, as curious as their elders were about him.

The boys were fine. They came in, asked their questions directly, then left. To one or two, those who seemed most congenial or who came back for a second visit, Tom offered a free sweet. He hoped this would encourage them to come back again, perhaps become friends. One of these boys was Robert — "not Bob or Bobby," he told Tom on first meeting, "Robert."

Robert was not like the other boys. To begin with, he actually, from time to time, had coin in his pocket and could pay for his sweets. He made a point of doing so after accepting only one free one from Tom.

Robert's clothes were always clean, his trousers always neatly pressed, he wore gold wire-rimmed glasses, and was as neat and clean at the end of the day as he was at the beginning. He wore braces always and a white shirt with the sleeves rolled to the elbows and a bow-tie and he had attended schools, had a quick smile and curly mousey-brown hair which he kept hidden under a salt-and-pepper cap.

His father, Tom was told, captained an ocean-crossing four-master out of Boston, a job of great importance and one held in high respect by the people on the Reach Run.

Because of the status conferred by his father, and despite the fact he was friendly enough, a distance was always maintained between Robert and other boys. Tom, however, presented an opportunity Robert had never had before. For even though Tom was taller and stronger and looked older than Robert, everyone knew they were, in fact, about the same age; and Tom worked indoors, mainly, at a responsible job and that raised him up to a slightly higher status than the rest of the boys. Tom was a friend Robert thought his father would approve of, and one Robert always knew he could find.

The young girls were a different matter. They first arrived being careful about how they looked — they took care to wear a nice dress, to make sure their hair was in place, then they took one long look at

Tom, his face corrupted, sore, tender-looking, constantly draining, and then as quickly as possible they bought whatever they needed and did not look him in the face again. After that they gave not another second of their thought as to how they looked when they had to go to the store.

Tom watched the young girls come and go but would not permit himself to feel anything at all about how they were treating him. He kept his feelings down and turned again to using the accounts books to occupy his mind.

One afternoon Tom was out back working when he heard a yelp from the front of the store, then laughter, and then the footfalls of two running about. When Tom came upon them, Robert was mischievously chasing a young woman around the store. She stopped running as soon as she saw Tom. She stood up straight, one hand on her hip, the other pressed between her breasts, which were impressive, and just now heaving mightily; her cheeks were flushed as she tried to catch her breath, but she was smiling. She was plain-looking and wore a simple green dress with a high collar. Her dress was the colour of her eyes, and her hair was long and black and pulled back from her face and loosely braided halfway down her back.

While she caught her breath, Robert turned around. "Tom!" he said, "This is . . . this is . . . my good friend . . . Elizabeth!"

"Not Liz," Elizabeth said archly, mocking Robert, "or Lizzie or Libby, but *E-liz-a-beth!*"

Tom smiled, Robert made as if to chase her again, she gave a playful scream and bolted from the store. Robert ran to the door and shouted after her, "I'll get you later, missy!" He laughed after her, nodded, waved, then shut the door and was smiling when he came back to Tom.

"That one is full of fun," he said.

A few days later she came to the store by herself, dressed just as before. Tom was busy with customers — wrapping everything he sold in brown paper, tying it up, and all the while chatting away about the pleasant weather and then recording the transactions. He had a sense of wherever Elizabeth went in the store, and he stole glances at her whenever he could. She walked slowly, unhurriedly, thoughtfully about, one hand cupping an elbow, the other on her chin.

When all the other customers were gone, Elizabeth walked towards him, then stopped and leaned against the pillar nearest his counter. She positioned her hands behind her to cushion her back, which thrust both her bosom and pelvis forward. Tom could not keep his eyes off her breasts.

"Well," Elizabeth said slowly, softly, "do you like it here?" She watched him carefully as he answered.

"It'll do for now, I guess," Tom said, reluctantly looking up.

Elizabeth nodded. She looked around, then back at him again. "Do you think you'll stay long?" she asked.

Tom shrugged.

"None of the others did," Elizabeth said, shaking her head. "None of them — did you know any of them, talk to any of them before you came up?"

"No."

Elizabeth nodded, pleased somehow with his answer. "I knew them all," she said. She pushed away from the pillar and walked to the counter, gripped its edge with both hands, so the heels of her hands and wrists faced Tom. She leaned across the counter and swayed just a little. Her breasts squeezed and strained against the fabric of her dress. Tom started to breathe shallowly, quickly, and he swallowed. Elizabeth looked up at him coquettishly, leaned ever closer. "I bet," she said with a sigh, "that I know places in this store that you haven't even found yet."

"Do you — " he stopped to clear his throat, "do you think so?"

"If we go out there," Elizabeth said, nodding to the storeroom, "I can show you."

Tom's heart was pounding. He nodded, tentatively at first, then with conviction and then he was able to say, "Well, let's see."

He led the way. She closed the first door behind them as Tom lifted the latch on the second and when he was in the doorway, she touched him on the shoulder. "Wait," she softly ordered, adding, "don't turn around."

All the while behind him, she slid the suspenders from his shoulders, pulled his shirt out of his trousers. Her hand went softly and smoothly across his stomach then down to touch, then quickly out to undo his trouser buttons, taking a second to press his hard and growing interest through the fabric, then her hand dove back inside where she now had room enough to grip him freely and pull him out into the open. Tom groaned, leaned against the door frame, eyes closed, her hand small and cool and stroking. With her other hand she was doing something, he did not know what but he could feel her movements on his back, and when he made a motion to look over his shoulder, she communicated to him through a moment's hesitation in her stroke and a gentle squeeze that he should not. He felt his shirt lift and then he felt the heat and knew that Elizabeth's bare breasts were pressed to his back. It was all more. All more than. More than he could hold, back. He groaned again. His seed shot, spilled, to the sawdust floor of the storeroom. And he had to reach down, hold her by the wrist before she would stop.

While they were getting themselves back in order, she told him not to turn around.

"But why not?" Tom asked. "I just — "

"Never you mind asking 'Why?'" Elizabeth said. "Just keep your back to me until I say so — *and NO! I mean it* — don't you dare try to steal a look. If you do, nothing like this will ever happen again."

"Okay," Tom said, nodding. After a moment he asked, "Is it because of me or you?"

"Both."

He was waiting a long time it seemed before she told him he could turn around.

She looked exactly as she had when she'd entered the store, not a hair out of place, as if nothing at all had happened.

"I - I - " Tom started, looking down and away and not knowing really what to say now that he was looking at her.

Elizabeth shook her head sternly. "Never mind that," she said. She squeezed past him in the doorway into the storeroom proper. She turned to the right and walked to a cabinet where several bolts of cloth were standing upright. She quickly and expertly examined them and then, with an effort, pulled one blue bolt up and out, laid it on a nearby measuring table, and unrolled a length. Then she stepped back, crossed her arms and eyed the cloth lovingly.

Tom looked from the cloth to Elizabeth then back to the cloth again, then back to Elizabeth. Finally he said, "Oh!" He looked around for a pair of scissors.

"This is very delicate cloth," Elizabeth said as he cut the length from the bolt for her. "It often is ruined in shipping — so I've been told by the others who have worked here. Has that been your experience, Tom?"

Tom nodded. "I'll mark it so in the book," Tom said. "You don't have to worry about it."

His heart would always pound when he saw her come into the store after that. And if she came to transact real business — to buy flour, sewing thread or kerosene — his heart would sink. But if she came when the store was quiet, he would be ready for her attention before they reached the storeroom door, and it was often over as quickly. Gladly, he always gave her a gift of her own choosing — fabrics and imported fruitcakes in tins and small porcelain ornaments were her favourites.

He thought nothing of repaying kindness with kindness.

As it had been that first time, so it was each time — she stood behind Tom, reached around, and she would have none of it if he attempted to turn. After enough time had passed for their meetings to take on an air of sweet familiarity, he could not help but wonder if, in truth, she simply could not bear to look at his boiling, roiling face.

"Elizabeth?" he said one afternoon.

"Yes?"

He coughed, his throat tight, his voice hoarse. "Don't you think it might be good fun for us to do, you know, a natural thing . . . *facing* each other?"

Elizabeth refused, flatly. "No — I don't do that," she said.

. . .

She walked into the store one day, head down and wearing a bonnet. As soon as Tom looked up and saw her, he smiled, but then she looked up, her left eye black and swollen shut but seeping a tear nonetheless. Following her into the store was a tall, powerful-looking man walking with a slow, purposeful stride. He had a long white beard combed out from his chin like a fan and he held his head high.

When Tom and Elizabeth's eyes met, she began to weep, then turned away, holding the handkerchief in her small hands to her face.

"Hush, child!" the man commanded in a voice that froze Tom to the counter with fear. Elizabeth went quiet quickly, her shoulders jumping from the effort to contain her sobbing. Tom knew then that this man was Elizabeth's father. He approached the counter slowly in his full height, radiating, it seemed to Tom, some kind of authority, and ready to dispense some kind of judgement.

He looked down at Tom and sternly said, "We will be having a Black Marriage."

Whatever was in Tom's bowels seemed to turn to water, but he was lucky and able to clamp off a sudden outflowing.

Elizabeth wailed.

"*Quiet!*" the father shouted over his shoulder.

But this time she could not control or contain herself and she ran from the store still sobbing. Tom saw her as she passed by a small window. He could no longer hear her crying but her face was unlike any he'd ever seen, a swollen, ugly, tortured mask of grief, and he could not help but wonder if others saw him that way.

"A Black Marriage for that one," the man said.

Alone, petrified, Tom turned his full attention to the man. "Sir?" he asked hoarsely. "A Black Marriage?"

"That one is with child and unwed, God forgive her, but she will be married, to the father — the young Robert." Tom's own fear left him quick-as-that. "Now, you must write a letter for me, to the minister, and we must hope that it will find him before a child is born in disgrace. It would be better if we could send it down the wire, but we've no sender."

"And no wire," Tom said as, hands trembling, he brought up writing paper.

"Oh yes," the man said, "we have a wire, a proper telegraph office, but senders and storekeepers are much alike — they do not stay up here for very long."

Tom nodded, then bent over the paper, pen in hand, and waited for the message to be dictated.

Tom hoped there would be others like Elizabeth, but there were not. Now, as before, even his mildest approaches to other girls were rejected, in disgust or disbelief.

Sometimes he wished that Elizabeth had never introduced him to the pleasure, for now he burned with a specific fire as he had never burned before — his fantasy had a face and a focus, his flesh a memory, and it seemed the more he fought his desire the more he was consumed by it, and when he met his own need, he felt a profound isolation.

When none of his own ministrations cleared his corrupted flesh, he remembered his mother's admonishment to remember God . . . so he prayed for his face to be cleansed. And soon, in long fervent sessions on his knees in his rooms at the back of the store, he was asking God to set all things right in his life, and without really thinking about it or questioning it at all, he slipped into praying for justice and a divine judgement, for vengeance against Edward Lank.

3

The telegrapher's office was a small cube of a building with a peaked roof, telegraph wires entering at one end, leaving from the other. There was a single door on one side, a single window on the other. But there was no telegrapher. As with the store, it was hard to find a qualified person who wanted to work in so isolated a place.

Tom wrote to St. John's and learned the position of telegrapher paid more than he was making running Lank's store. So he wrote again, this time in application, and was quickly accepted as a trainee in the six-week telegrapher's course, which he would have to take in St. John's, and on condition that he would return and work on the Reach Run for at least one year.

On his last day in the store, he was visited by the same two fishermen who, on the first day, had wanted to see him add and subtract and make out a bill. When Tom told them he'd be working there no more, they managed to mumble "Goodbye." It seemed to Tom his leaving concerned them even less than his arrival. They knew him as little, he realized, as he knew them.

First thing back in St. John's, he handed his letter of resignation to Lank's secretary and left. He had no desire to see or to speak to Edward Lank ever again.

To the surprise of the half dozen men in telegrapher training, a girl was also taking the course. Beautiful eyes, Tom thought right away. She looked at him only once.

He visited his old home but had no desire to go in. In the year since he'd seen it last a few windows had been smashed out and boarded up, steps had split and gone unrepaired, garbage had piled up around the foundation and decayed, and parts of the house were badly in need of paint. He found it hard to believe that anyone lived there, and paid rent to Lank, who'd bought the house as a favour to Tom when he went North. Because that money was his inheritance, Tom kept it safe and untouched in the bank.

He visited the graves, and because he did not know when he'd be back in St. John's again, he went in the evening and pulled weeds and washed the small headstones. He took away, in separate little bottles, pieces of earth from each of the plots.

When he started his new work, he kept the earth in the night table by the side of his boardinghouse bed.

While he was away Robert and Elizabeth had married and moved. To Boston, it was said, but no one was really sure.

Tom's face and loins burned. His face felt as if it were in rebellion against itself, as if lumps and bumps could not agree on shape, his face always infected, red and sore.

He worked alone, sending and receiving messages, but all the while he just couldn't get the young women out of his head, was often beside himself with a need to be near them. Accidentally touching a woman's hand as he passed a message under the wicket was often enough to inflame his thoughts. And some of the young women were wickedly naughty, teasing. They spoke to him suggestively, he thought, or, perhaps, hoped. They hinted that they knew all about his times with Elizabeth, and they winked at him, and that stoked both his imagination and his sexual desires. In dreams, the unyielding, unknown folds of female flesh somehow managed to coax substance out of him.

He caged his desire behind the wicket of the telegrapher's office. He worked long hours so as not to have time on his hands. Often, late at night, the key would query. Tom would respond, then take and send the backlog of messages. He was a skilful sender, had a good ear and good writing skills too, so as he interpreted and transcribed the dots and dashes, his mind sometimes wandered — he'd imagine signals speeding through wires. He knew the telegraph company's

office on Water Street, and could imagine himself hovering above
that office, then jumping a signal on the line, imagine the zip from
city lights into the deep dark. He would crackle down lines alongside
moonlit ponds, lakes, would zing up hills, down valleys, zigzag
through fields, the windows of farmhouses square in the night —
and suddenly he'd see the country entire, as if suspended above,
seeing all at once: wilderness — rock, forest and pond — lights on
the coast, the sea.

In the summer of 1892, the city of St. John's, including the Lank
foundry and the house where Tom was born, burnt to the ground.

Years later Hammond Janes would recount his childhood
memories of that Great Fire for Tom. If they were not Hammond's
earliest memories of his childhood, they were certainly the strongest.
He was just six years old, and as his father hurried him out of the
house that July day, Hammond snatched the slate and chalk he used
in school.

Later, from the safety of a high hill, he watched the monster
blaze. Whipped by high and dry summer winds, it roared and
crackled out in all directions, it ravaged and consumed and transformed the city to a great and rising column of heat and thick smoke.
Hammond thought of nothing at all. He drew simple pictures on his
slate, erasing them with the heel of his hand as soon as they were
done: houses on fire were easy to do — squares with flames in the
windows, with fire dancing on the roof; the hundreds, *the thousands*, of
people scurrying before the flames were more difficult — he
crowded his slate with heads and shoulders, their only features being
wide-open eyes, wide-open mouths; for smoke he laid the chalk on
its side and swirled until every bit of slate was covered, and then, for
the sun, he used his little finger to clear a spot high in the corner.

He fell asleep watching the creature leap into the night and next
morning it had escaped, had leapt finally, he imagined, over the
Southside Hills and away. The signs of its passage, the only things
standing in the ashes: stone fireplaces and chimneys, as if deliberately
left for markers.

. . .

Tom Vincent, sixteen-year-old telegrapher on the Reach Run, received the news of the great conflagration as one whose prayers have been answered, his father's death avenged.

Then a great guilt.

How many homeless? Injured? Dead? The questions he tapped out. *All unknown*, the answer came back.

He set his pads aside, blew out the lanterns, locked the office door and walked home to his boardinghouse.

It was a quiet evening — a mackerel sky.

He slept fitfully, unable to rid himself of the thought that his life had suddenly gone off at an angle, somehow forever altered from a true and natural course.

When he got to work the next morning, a crowd was already waiting, anxious for news out of St. John's. He had just settled down to his desk when the key began. Tom told them there was an appeal for donations of clothing and footwear of all sizes. "Twelve thousand ... homeless ... and in desperate need," he went on. A good number of that twelve thousand, Tom reported, conscious always of things eternal had gathered that very morning " . . . to sing hymns . . . to kneel in the ashes . . . to thank God there'd been no loss of life." And Tom, silently, without missing a letter of the transcription, offered up his own prayer of thanksgiving for the vengeance that had come sure and certain, but in which no one had suffered a death.

Later, when Tom heard that the Reverend Hollis Harris would be holding a service down in Herring Neck, he travelled, for the first time, from Reach Run Island to the Neck.

There, beneath a cloudless sky on a warm Sunday morning at the ocean's very edge, Tom chose to be baptized again, to be born again in Christ. Standing with the cold saltwater up to his armpits, Tom pinched his nostrils together. And standing there right alongside him, Reverend Harris, hair red and tangly as hellfire, put his hand on the back of Tom's head and pushed him under. Tom came out of the water smiling. He looked around at the men and women from settlements all up and down the coast, and they all smiled back at him, welcomed and congratulated him with handshakes and slaps on the back. It was as if he'd found family again.

He joined their Christian Men's Organization that day and took a copy of their constitution back to Reach Run Island with him.

From then on, Tom made it his practice to attend church in the Neck the first Sunday of every month. A month after baptism his face had become dry and scaly. Within six months, all the infections cleared, his face left generally and deeply scarred.

PART II

I

Thickets of juniper and dwarf white birch grew on a tract of nearly level land Tom crossed every day on his way to and from work. He had the notion that the land could be cultivated.

One evening he stepped off the path, crouched, tore through shrubs and matted moss to pull up handfuls of soil, black and moist. He liked the feel of it squeezing through his fingers. It had a good smell when he held it to his nose.

Rolling the soil off his hands, he stood and looked about. It was the northerly exposure, he guessed, that had kept others away.

Further back, he discovered a small stream. A very good thing, he thought. He decided to take the chance.

With just a little of his inheritance, he was able to buy the neglected freehold land.

Before his first planting he stood in his field with the two bottles of soil from the graves of his mother and father. As if casting seed he emptied them on his own ground.

From the very first season, he had a surplus of produce which he arranged to sell on a cash-only basis to the new man running Lank's store.

Tom then used that cash to buy from the store the tools and whatever else he needed. He bought nothing on credit.

In time, as his yields increased and he had even more cabbage and carrot and turnip and potato to sell, he developed, on a small scale, a cash-only trade with the schoonermen. They were always on the lookout for a supply of good fresh vegetables, and sometimes they bought from him in bulk. Despite being off the beaten track and operating only with cash, Tom prospered a little and, all in all, was comfortable with his living. Because he only took cash, however, the majority of fishermen did no business with him at all.

He built a two-storey house of modest proportion, and later, when he could afford it, added on a large room. He silently named this room 'The Store,' and from then on he conducted all his business there. By this time he had confidence enough in his abilities as a farmer to end his career as a telegrapher in order to devote all his energies to farming.

For fifteen years Tom farmed on Reach Run Island.

Take the best part of every season, he told Hammond Janes, string them all together in proper order, and you would have the perfect season.

You had to know a thousand things. By the day and by the season, you had to know weather and time by natural signs; and when to plant and when to reap; and how to trench the soil, and how to feed it with kelp and capelin; and only after years would you know which vegetables took in lobster shells, and were sweeter for it, and suchlike and so on, on and on, a thousand things or more.

In the perfect season, as Tom envisioned it, he would plant neither too early nor too late, and frost would be no problem coming or going, and midsummer would pass without storms of wind, rain or hail. Over the years he had made those mistakes and all those things had happened. In his perfect season he would recognize the early signs of peril in perforation of leaf, droop of stem, or dryness of soil. He would know, right away, what he had to do to save his crop. He would have the special experience of his land to answer whatever it asked of him, not just for the sake of good vegetables, or for the pleasure of perfected process, but as one who fit the Earth where he was, in fraternity with trees, soil and rocks.

As Tom lived out these years of his life on this land, he did not hesitate to talk to it, for he saw rocks, soil, crops and trees as personalities that he could, up to a point, coax, cajole, and wheedle into doing as he wanted. Sometimes, when all was in fullness of growth, he wondered if he were anything without them, and that was a satisfying thought. Through the Earth he sensed a nearness to ancient mysteries which he understood in no way that could be spoken or written, but of which he felt the truth, and sacredness, as he lived out his part on the land, both taking and creating from it.

The Earth, the sea, the soil, the trees — none of them ever at rest, a restless imperative. Running through the unchanging, a power of transformation.

At the end of some summer days he stood in awe of the setting sun. In the field, he stood holding a spade in one hand, while his free hand shaded his eyes. Skies singularly tinted, red or orange, on some days; on other days, as mad and majestic a plurality of colour as anyone would ever see.

Without his witness, he believed, these moments would have no existence at all.

Across the evening skies of summer he marked the transit of Jupiter, and wondered how many other men down through time had looked to the Father of the Sky for some sign of destiny.

Tom prided himself on his patient attitude. And, over the years, his reward came in the continuing resonance of his wonder.

Out of these years also come the first stories of Tom as a physician of sorts, of his unusual knowledge and method.

He was in the field and there was a queer and sudden twist in the sun, so it seemed, and a pain screwed through the skull above the right temple to the very brain and lodged just above and behind his right eye. "*Christ!*" he exclaimed at the suddenness and the pain of it and he shook his head to shake it away and closed his eyes but it would not disappear. He knelt down on one knee to rest and to hang his head a moment, determined to continue his work from there, on his knees if he could not do it on both feet. He cursed himself and his weakness and with more effort than he thought it would require he stood, but only for a moment, for everything began to fade before his eyes and he stumbled face-first into his plants and he could smell the earth and the green and he could feel the sun on his neck — all these familiar things — and this foreign icepick sharpness stabbing into his head and he knew if he did not move then it might be some time before he could move again. He rolled over on his back and the sun on his face intensified his pain somehow and to avoid that direct heat he grimaced and pushed himself up until he was sitting, head hanging, hands on his knees. Very cautiously he twisted until he was on his knees, then he planted a foot on the ground, stood slowly, and when that was accomplished, he walked slowly down the field between the rows, then up the steps, and opened his door. He was in the coolness of his kitchen then and he had a thought of the soft feather bed upstairs but chose instead the kitchen daybed because he could go no further and he fell on it on his side, the thought of the bed upstairs stuck in his mind, as if the very next moment he would get up and go there, but he had neither will nor strength to power himself up.

He was aware at some level of all the day's work going undone, of everything being left as it was, of a day interrupted, of everything waiting — he was aware of time passing. He would close his eyes and open them again and all would be the same in the kitchen except for the way the light angled to it, and touched it and then it was dark and he knew there were doors to be closed and latched for the night, lanterns to be lit, a stove to be fired up — a chill slid across the floor, rose up the walls, and fell on everything. Night breezes in the trees outside. Very late he turned over on his back and lay there for a very long time with his eyes open but thinking of nothing but his breathing.

But when he tried to sit, the pain bore into his head and laid him out again, one eyelid fluttered, flashes of red and elliptical yellows appeared and disappeared before his eyes.

It was a long while — near dawn — before he tried to move again, and although he was able to sit without dramatic consequence, the pain in his head intensified to throb and to pound, and he felt weak for being unable to rid himself of it, and he made fists and pressed them to his temples but the pain implacably persisted.

He stood and, slowly, without knowing why, he wandered out of his house into the cool dawn air, then across his fields and into the trees. With his nails, he scraped, picked and tore at the bark of a spruce and when he had wrenched and twisted a sticky strip away he was breathing heavily and sweating. He put one end into his mouth, chewed on it for a time trying to suck the sap out of it, remembering then that somewhere he had read that the sap of certain trees in Europe had medicinal properties, had the property to deaden pain, but the sap of the spruce had no such power and by noon the pain had driven Tom, in desperation, through the forest to seek help from his nearest neighbour.

Caught just sitting down to dinner, John Sutton and his wife helped Tom to their daybed, Tom babbling on that he was sick, with a headache. The farmer was a tall, thin man who always wore a hat out of doors. He had a pale bald crown atop a sunburned face and neck. He told his wife to bring the vinegar plant and brown wrapping paper and saucers. Her face had been the picture of worry until her husband gave her something to do.

She brought him a large cork-stoppered glassen jar. In it a thick brown raft of scum floated on clear liquid. By the time his wife came back with the crackling paper, he had uncorked the jar and the air was filled with a sour sharpness released when he pushed the covering scum to one side, and his hand was up, reaching for the paper even before she arrived. He tore off a long narrow strip which he then folded end over end and dipped into the vinegar. When it was well-soaked, he lifted it out and applied it to Tom's forehead. As cool and soothing as the compress was, the sharp odour was equally curative, for the first breath of it brought tears to his eyes, the tartness seeming to pierce right through to the pain. There was momentary relief, and Tom breathed deeply of it again. After a time and after a certain number of applications, the pain was much diminished. When Tom fell asleep, they covered him with a heavy blanket. Tom spent a second day and night on a daybed. When he awoke the next morning the headache was gone and he had a ravenous appetite. The Suttons fed him.

Tom learned from them how to grow his own vinegar plant — molasses and water in a bottle, stoppered tight and kept warm near the stove. In a month it soured, then the plant formed and the vinegar would be made, simple as that. Tom wanted to know what other properties it had, besides being a cure for headaches, and he wanted to know all of what they knew of medicines, wanted to know because he was alone on his farm and would need such knowledge to take care of himself, so they talked to him about Radway's Ready Relief and Ginger Wine, and the little pills from Carter and Dodd, and Sweet Spirits of Nitre. They showed him their precious and blessed Friars' Balsam ointment, and camphorated oil and told how a few drops of the Minard's boiled into a molasses taffy could be bitten off and sucked on for relief from winter colds.

From then on, he inquired of all those he had occasion to visit as to what remedies for ailments they might know. Because he asked the questions, he was soon known as one with an interest in such matters. People freely offered him their medicinal wisdom, and Tom took it all in. It was not long before people were making the long walk to his farm to take *his* counsel since he had come to know in whole what others knew only in part.

Most said they benefited from his advice, willingly and gladly given. But he also came to be known for the ire in his voice and the quickness of his manner, second time around, if you chose, in the first instance, not to follow his instructions.

He experimented on himself with mushrooms, plants and berries, and with the bark and roots of trees, singly and in combinations — this one he discovered was a powerful purgative, these a potent emetic, and those mushrooms lifted you up on a wave of nausea and left you in a wake of dreams — he kept what worked.

Of the thousand things or more he knew how to do, Tom most loved to dig potatoes in the fall — reds, blues and the big "Scotch Apples."

As the sun angled away to its winter region, an uneasiness would rise in him, lasting until winter weather had come for sure, and he had adjusted to interior time.

In winter the cold seemed to enlarge the night skies. And when conditions were right, cold and clear, on winter nights, Tom made it a practice to stand in the middle of his snow-covered fields and look up to mighty Orion. He marvelled at the great expanse of sky that giant constellation claimed.

Reading, rest and repair work were never enough to fill the whole of winter.

Invariably, his thoughts turned to the fishermen.

While he harvested his vegetables and was making a good go of it as farmer-businessman, they harvested fish and were all indebted to merchantmen, who kept fish low and flour high. A simple enough problem but challenging too. As winters wore on it kept his mind occupied.

No single time, no single thread; an evolution.

What the fishermen needed, Tom came to believe, was someone separate or different from themselves who yet understood them and could see what needed to be done in the fishery. They would find it difficult to follow one of their own, but they might be able to rally around someone who stood apart.

Tom met George Gill, ordinary seaman, one summer afternoon on Reach Run Island. The skipper of George's schooner was too busy to make a visit himself, so he sent George to deliver two books to Tom.

Tom was out back when he heard the bell ring. George stood there, looking about, the two books in his hand.

"Those," Tom said, smiling, "must be for me."

"If you're Tom Vincent," George said bluntly. He was a young man with broad shoulders and muscular arms. His eyes were clear, quick and bright.

"Right," Tom said. Nodding towards the books, "What titles?"

George looked at the books as if they were two lumps of coal, looked back at Tom. "Don't know," he answered. Tom came around the counter wide of the barrels of foodstuff. It was a narrow space, well lit with windows both sides of the door, but there was no extra room.

Tom took the books, checked the spines as he walked back behind the counter. "Good," he said under his breath. He gave

George the money owing, added some coin for the delivery, and George stood there, saying nothing at all.

"I'll go now," he said finally. When he opened the door, the bell rang again.

"Wait," Tom said, "a cup of tea before you go?"

George looked over his shoulder, hesitating.

"No charge," Tom added, smiling.

George nodded.

"Good!" Tom said.

Tom led George back to the kitchen, made the tea.

George sat at the kitchen table, quiet mostly, waiting.

"You're young to be on the schooners, George."

"Gotta work."

"Where you from?"

"Our Island."

"Do I know any Gills from Our Island?" Tom mused.

"None o' my family," George said. "My mother and father are dead and buried for years. I never knew them. Best that way I s'pose — I mean if they're going to die on you anyway."

"Perhaps you're right," Tom said. He thought of his own mother and father, George's words touching his heart in those very places.

George had not much in the way of manners, but Tom was patient with him, interested in him, and while he served the buns and biscuits he got George's story out of him — a little bit that first day, more and more on the visits that followed.

George was born on Our Island. His mother died birthing him, and when he was four his father, a fisherman, died of 'congestion on the lungs.' He was taken in by the Isaacs, a distantly related family of eight, six boys who were described by Islanders, when they were being kind, as tougher than pieces of old leather. The Isaac boys were all older and bigger than George and were almost always scrapping. They were loud and bitter with one another, and George soon learned to do nothing to attract attention to himself. Whenever attention was paid to anyone in that family, for whatever reason, it always ended in a racket. George did what he had to do to take care of himself, and because he was afraid, that meant he did as he was told.

He never felt part of the family — not that he was treated any differently than the other boys in terms of food to eat or clothes to wear, but they always spoke of him as 'poor Georgie' and he was never allowed to forget that he had been taken in. They teased him all the time by wondering out loud where he'd be now if it hadn't been for their kindness.

They were a family of fishermen. They had three boats and George felt most at ease with the boys when they were around their boats. They all knew their work, were changed beings, less contrary and rancorous, when they were at nets and fish, and what George cherished was that they asked him to do things, trusted him to do things. "George, pass down the knife." "Georgie, the rope..." and in doing those things George would become one of them.

Luke was George's favourite. He was the oldest, strongest and most likeable. He had blond curly hair, blue eyes and a beard. He smoked or chewed all the time and tobacco juice had stained his light-haired beard at the corners of his mouth. Luke taught George to split fish, and even built a small splitting table especially for him.

Standing at that table helping Luke gut the fish was the happiest time for George. George longed for the time when he'd be old enough to go fishing himself.

But that did not happen, not as George thought it would anyway.

When George was eight he was shipped across the island to live with Ned and Em Curtis, a childless couple. Ned and Em were not well. They suffered from a variety of complaints that George never fully understood. They were never without a pain, and never had energy enough to do anything. They felt very bad, needed help, so they'd talked to the Isaacs to see if they would let George go, let him come live with them, to help out around the house. George was not the Isaacs' own, Ned and Em had pleaded, and God knows with six sons, the Isaacs had plenty of mouths to feed, and Ned and Em would surely give the boy a good upbringing.

Scared though he had been for much of his time at the Isaacs, George had discovered parts of life that could be enjoyed and soon these were the very pleasures denied him. Being outdoors, being around boats and gardens and the boys were the main things. And smoking. And he loved the gathering of fishermen, their talk of fish and weather.

The Curtises were pale and their house was dark. They invited no visitors. They opened no windows. Allowed no smoking. Did not permit George to go out, except to Woolfrey's for groceries. They explained there was "nothing else to go out for." He'd just get his clothes dirty and nobody knew when anybody would be strong enough to do a wash of clothes again and when they tried to convince him of the virtues of being inside — George knew better and simply stopped listening.

George was responsible for everything from helping Em to the outhouse to shining Ned's shoes for Sunday services, church being the one, the only, place Ned and Em could be seen together outside of their house. George had to go to church with them, as part of his 'good upbringing.' After several weeks he realized that the Curtises were not so much living as waiting for the coming of the new day as he heard it proclaimed in church.

Four months later George met Luke at Woolfrey's. Luke told George he was missed down on the wharf and that he looked pale. Luke rolled him a smoke, George's first in ages.

That very afternoon saw his rebellion. It was short lived and simple, but it had a profound effect.

George went through the Curtis's house and swung all the windows open. Then, for show, he knocked over a piece of furniture and tore a picture off the wall, damaging neither, but most of all he just generally terrorized Ned and Em by shouting and cursing at them. They weakly screamed then weakly whined for him to stop, but he would not. Not until he was ready, and then he went out. For good.

Before long a smiling Luke came trudging down to the wharf with George's two small suitcases. The Curtises had thrown him back. All the Isaac boys cheered.

"That's some fight you got in you when you're roused up!" Luke said.

George nodded shyly, uncomfortable as the centre of attention, then he turned away to fiddle with an old piece of rope. Now that he was back, he wanted things to be as they were before. He would do what they wanted, and do nothing that might draw attention to himself.

Not many weeks later, Luke went out to his nets one morning. Though they later recovered his empty boat, they never found Luke.

George first went fishing when he was twelve. That was all there was for him to do. If he didn't know fishing, he'd know nothing.

After the first few summers, he was expected to pay his own way at the Isaacs, and he did. When he had a chance to work on a Woolfrey schooner, he took it, and after that, except for the occasional visit to the Isaacs out of courtesy for what they had done in taking him in, taking him in twice really, he had no ties to anybody.

On the schooners, he travelled the coasts. He worked hard, learned his work quickly, and he felt things would continue as they were going, perhaps forever. And that was good because, for the first time in his life, he knew the feel of his own money in his own pocket.

When George had done talking and eating that first day on Reach Run Island, he stood up, wishing he could stay longer, and walked out without a word of thanks.

Tom leaned on the door frame as George began the walk back. "George," Tom called after him, and George stopped.

Tom nodded in another direction, "That way."

"T'anks," George said, and tramped off.

He became a regular visitor, went to see Tom even if he had no business, no books to deliver. Tom might later be known for his speech making, but when George knew him first he knew how to listen.

In the summer of 1907, Tom decided he needed to fish for at least a season, and the first thing he did was to hire George Gill.

George took a spare room in Tom's house.

2

Tom fared no better, no worse, than other fishermen. Likewise he could be set neither higher nor lower than the rest of the farmers on Reach Run Island. But Tom was fisherman and farmer both and what Tom had that others did not, as far as George could see, was simply the ability to organize. His days, weeks, and months were planned as if in the service of some greater scheme of things that only Tom knew.

In these plans Tom had definite roles for George to play, the main one being as his advisor on all things practical related to codfishing, but he still expected George to work the same as he himself worked, which was steadily and hard, properly, thoroughly.

Besides hard work and organization, George believed Tom had luck on his side too. Some days, for no reason George ever knew, and sometimes even against George's counsel, Tom would decide to leave early for the fishing grounds, and they'd find themselves back home with a boatload of fish just as the weather was coming up. Other boats would be coming back with their work only half done.

On land and on the sea, they hardly ever spoke to one another as they worked.

The first evening George spent in Tom's home, Tom asked him to start a fire. George grabbed some newspaper from a small stack at the end of the daybed. He crumpled it up, was about to drop it in the stove, when Tom held him gently but firmly by the wrist.

"No," Tom said. "Give it to me."

Surprised, puzzled, George handed the paper to him. Tom laid the crumbled ball on the kitchen table, opened it up and took care to smooth it out. As he did so he explained to George that *this* paper was for reading.

"Come with me," Tom said.

Upstairs, he opened a door to a room where there were shelves of books on every wall. Books. All shapes, sizes and conditions. Fifteen years of reading.

"Books," Tom said, motioning with his hand as if by way of introduction. "You cannot read," he said, looking at George.

"No sir."

"Well, I can teach you to read if you would like. Would you like that?"

George nodded.

"Can you do sums, can you calculate — add, subtract, divide?"

George shook his head.

"Then I can teach you something about figures, too! In the evening, when our work's done, we'll spend a little time reading and writing and working with numbers."

George had been living in Tom's house only a few weeks when Tom left early one Saturday morning to do some business down in Herring Neck.

George had never before been left alone in the house for any length of time.

He wandered into all the rooms, looking, but he touched nothing. On Saturday afternoon, he sat on the daybed; a little later, he lay down.

When he woke up, it was dark and cold so he put a fire in, cooked himself something to eat, and so that day was done, and likewise he whiled away Sunday and Monday, too.

When Tom came back late Monday night, he could see that nothing had been done, and George asleep upstairs.

Tom banged the door open, walked in. George up on an elbow, shielding his eyes from the light. Tom turned, laid the lantern on the dresser. He was wearing a long coat. When he moved, dark shadows stalked the walls.

"There's no wood in the wood box," Tom said, his back to George. "And you haven't touched the net. Well, you haven't touched anything, have you?"

"No sir," George answered.

Tom twirled around and the shadows on the walls and ceilings rearranged, massively.

"What have you done, son?" Tom asked quietly.

"Nothing," George said. "I — "

"Nothing!"

"I — "

"Why is that, George?"

"I — "

There was a sudden convulsion of shadow, and Tom loomed up next to George's bed. He yanked a chair over and sat. He leaned forward to face George. "That's not good enough, George. I've got to be able to rely on you. You should have carried on."

"But you weren't here," George protested. "It's your place and you weren't here to tell me what to do."

"Ahhh, boy," Tom said, "stop yer whining and listen to me." He sat up straight. The light at his back now, half the room was shadow. "And listen good because I'll only be telling you the once. This is not a schooner. You don't need to wait for an order before you do anything. The good helper," he said slowly, "the good lieutenant, is the one who sees what needs to be done, and does it regardless. Do you understand that, George?"

"Yes sir."

"Good!" Tom said. "Don't forget it."

"No sir."

Tom rose, the shadows went crazy, and Tom sucked them through the door with his light.

The season Tom and George fished together, all fishermen were lucky. It was the best fishing they'd had in years. They joked that Tom had brought them all the luck.

But the good fortune extended only so far. The price Lank paid for fish started high but soon fell, fell lower than it had been in years.

Tom and George worked hard all that summer, and though the boat was low in the water day after day, they soon knew they could not get ahead selling fish, for the price of fish stayed rock bottom, but the price of goods and gear crept up by a few pennies every week.

Looking for a way out, they travelled down the coast to Our Island, to the nearest Woolfrey store, but prices there were as bad as they were on Reach Run.

During this visit to Our Island, George heard Tom talk union, in the normal course of conversation, to some fishermen there on a wharf, but he paid it no mind at the time.

In late October Tom and George gave up the fishing. Tom used the bills and receipts of their season's work as a practical arithmetic lesson. They added up expenses; they added up income; they compared the two figures.

They owed money.

"Imagine," Tom said, "if we now had to buy winter provisions. Imagine if we carried over debts from other years. *That* is the fishermen's problem."

Then, as if imagining those very things, Tom sank into a gloom that lasted a week.

One afternoon, he rose up and said they had work to do.

In the kitchen, using the price that fish had fetched early in their season, Tom calculated the amount of money they'd have made if that price had held. Then he paid George one third of that amount, in cash, from a thick roll of bills he pulled out of a pocket.

"One third of nothing is nothing, which is what we made from the fishing," Tom said. "But no man will work with me for nothing."

George looked at the money on the table.

"Well, take it," Tom said. "And thank God the farming pays for our fishing."

George took it up, looked at it.

"Now," Tom said, "we'll go to Lank's."

They squared their bill there.

When they got home, Tom spent most of the next few days at the kitchen table, writing.

When he finished, he telegraphed down to Herring Neck that he would soon need the use of the parish hall for one, maybe two, nights.

3

From his farm on Reach Run Island to Herring Neck, walking through the white spruce forests over hills and down around the ponds, was a day's labour.

He'd called the public meeting in Herring Neck's parish hall for the second of November, at seven o'clock in the evening.

Unexpectedly he was called out to staunch an unstoppable nosebleed, which he accomplished with a plug of frankum and spiderweb, so he started out for Herring Neck later than he'd planned on the afternoon of November the first — but this was nothing to him, for he would just as soon travel by night as by day.

That year in the northern parts of Newfoundland the last days of October had gone storming out unseasonably and November had come in on a snap of deep and bitter cold. Ponds had frozen but not to any depth and a layer of icy sifted snow was everywhere. Tom was anxious for the weather to hold. As long as the cold held he'd take the chance on skipping across the ponds on soft sinking ice rather than walking the tangly paths around, and with the journey that much straightened, his progress was as efficient as he could have it.

In the knapsack on his back he carried all he needed of food and clothing and other supplies, and at the bottom of the pack was a leather cylinder protecting the document he'd written, a draft of a constitution for a fishermen's union he hoped to found at the public meeting. He'd used the Constitution of the Christian Men's Organization as a guide. The document he carried was handwritten and composed of his own thoughts on the needs and problems of fishermen.

He was walking now with a good travelling sweat and there was a rhythm to his breathing. As gray clouds sank lower and turned a shade darker his mind graced him with the image of a great wheel. Suspended somewhere was a great silver wheel in a slow turn, and so much depended on where you caught that wheel: here on the rise or there in descent. As the sound of snow sliding off his boots hissed in his ears he thought that given time enough he'd travel the great wheel all the way round and come to know all positions and oppositions — he'd see the pure, and the pure corrupted, and corruption purified yet again with further turning of the wheel.

When it became dark he heard wind in the trees and the wind carried a storm on its back and after a time on account of the driven snow he had to stop. He cut small wood and boughs for a lean-to, and also used a canvas sheet he'd brought for just such a purpose.

The wind soon drifted snow over the shelter and he was snug enough there and with the storm hard and unrelenting above he dropped into thinking again that the trajectory of the individual life depends on where you catch that wheel. On that stormy November night in 1908, he felt in the fullness of physical well-being. The thought that he was attempting a mighty thing filled him with a vigour that rushed through his head opening up corridors of possibility. Some of those corridors had a palpable quality, a certainty, as if he were feeling into the future. That November evening, he was catching the wheel on the rise. He kept a fire going all night.

Overnight the storm blew itself out. The dawning sky was cloudless.

Light came to the earth like golden liquid, snow was thickly clotted in the trees.

4 When Tom Vincent stood to speak, there was not an empty chair in the hall, and people were standing in the back. Outside it was cold and clear but blowing a gale, and from where Tom stood on the stage looking out through a window down into the valley, he could make out the shape of the church, all dark and quiet.

The wind whistled into the hall all evening and gave the lantern light the fits.

Tom was wearing his best suit and a tie, and his speech was rolled up tightly behind his back. But he knew as he looked out on that crowd of fishermen that it would be a mistake to deliver a prepared speech. How to begin?

Without another thought, he launched into it.

"I want to talk to you tonight," he said, "about setting up a union for fishermen. I am telling you this straight out, my friends, because there's no other way to tell you. I could fool around it for a while but when you come down to it, that is the reason for this meeting. The union I see will be as honest and straightforward as I am being with you right now. Now each man has his thoughts on this matter I am sure, so those of you who do not want to hear this, you do not have to stay. Those of you willing to hear me out will be courteous enough to wait a few minutes for the others to leave."

No one left. So he knew he'd made a good beginning. And he got halfway through what else he had to say before he was challenged from the floor.

"Sounds like to me that you're calling us lazy and stupid," one fellow shouted.

"No," Tom answered. "What I am saying is exactly contrary.

The issue is not laziness but strength. You — *we* — we do not yet know how strong we are. And as for stupid: if our stomachs go empty while others eat their fill from the profits of our labour, and if we continue to live in debt, forever in truck to the merchantman, even *after* we know it could be different, know there could be food in *our* bellies and money in our own pockets, why then yes, I guess that would be stupid, wouldn't it? But I do not believe that will be the case — hear me out. If I believed it had to be that way, I would not be here tonight trying to make a union. For to make a union is hard work and smart work and I am here because I know we are not afraid of hard work and because I know we are smart enough to know when something is wrong. And something is wrong when we have a grand season for fish yet none can make a go of it."

There was some applause. The crowd motioned for the fellow to sit. But as he sat he shouted, "We've had unions before and gotten nowhere."

"Oh," Tom said, "it will be a difficult thing to do, lads. Who will want it besides the fishermen? Not the men who buy our fish, for sure. It is likely that when they discover there is a union and that you are part of it, it is likely then that they will not buy your fish or sell you anything. That is what they have done in the past."

The same fellow jumped to his feet. "That's the end of it then, isn't it?" he shouted.

"NO!" Tom shouted back, the first time he'd raised his voice all evening. "No. Not the end. A beginning, perhaps. If there are enough of us, if we stand together as one, I think we will be able to set up our own trading company and there we will sell whatever the merchants refuse. This union will be different. We will be ready when the merchantman closes his book on us. This time we will oblige neither merchantman nor politician by fading away, and by the time they know this, it will be too late for them to do anything to stop us. But our main problem now, as I see it, is very simple — the price of fish is too low. The solution is simple enough, too — a better price for fish, and the best way to get that price is for all to act as one and to speak with the one collective voice, clear and determined not to sell fish for any price less than the best . . ."

At the end of his speech Tom went back to what he'd been hammering home all evening: "Fishermen must speak for fishermen. Fishermen, UNITE!" he shouted. "Fishermen," he then said quietly, "unite."

Later they voted, and all were agreed. The Fishermen's Collective was founded that very night. Tom's constitution was ratified and Herring Neck was given

The Instrument of Authority
Number One
To Establish and Work a Local Council

and Tom signed that document as the first President of the Collective.

They kept him talking on then in a rambly way for half the night, wanting the particulars of the future he saw for the fishermen, and when the meeting was over they burst out of the hall into the night and the night was clear, the stars shining, and the wind had died down and the moon was high. More than a few people were surprised when they stepped out to discover that all was much the same as before the meeting, as if, somehow, they had fully expected that Tom's visions would already have come to pass.

The following afternoon as Tom was out walking he met up with a merchantman out walking, too. Tom did not recognize the man to call him by name but by his manner and bearing and the cut of his fine clothes Tom knew what he was, and the last thing he expected was that the merchantman would call him by name. But call out he did.

"Mr. Vincent!" he said.

"Yes?" Tom replied, and the merchantman huffed and lifted his chin and looked down his nose at him. Tom was curious enough to walk over to him anyway. The merchantman had his lips pressed tightly together.

"Who called you to your work?"

Tom looked back at him straight. "Sir," he said, "just to see and to know is call enough."

. . .

The rest of that fall and winter Tom was up and down the coast. The fishermen took him across tickle and bay alike, made sure he had a place to speak, be it parish hall, church, or kitchen. It made no difference to him.

Then, through public speaking sometimes two or three times a day, he noticed something, something not in the words of his speeches, but in the silences between words and sentences. Whatever it was it crackled with an energy like lightning and it was full of tendency and direction and it would drift away if Tom did not guide it, and Tom found that the right words to do this always came to him with ease, like gifts.

The people fed him well and made sure he had warm dry comfortable places to sleep. They gave him clothes. Stocking caps and trigger mitts and woolen socks. One woman knit a blue guernsey for him and at the very next meeting he surrendered shirt and tie to wear the guernsey instead. At the following meeting he wore the same again, but, for a decoration, he had added a patch made in the shape of a codfish, had it sewn on the guernsey over his heart and that was how the figure of the white cod on the blue ground came to stand for the Fishermen's Collective.

From then on, wherever he went, there would always be some in the crowd wearing blue guernseys and codfish patches. Soon there were flags, too, and by the next summer they were flying on boats and houses all along what people now started to call 'The Collective Coast.'

In every place he visited, he encouraged those, if any, who could read and write, to write to government members to tell them about the Fishermen's Collective, its aims and purposes, and to ask where they stood on issues of the day — the grading and price of fish, for example. In no case did anyone ever receive a reply.

Early on the people learned other things about Tom: that he could charm a toothache away, could rid a person of warts, that he knew whether or not to lance a boil, could do it himself if need be, and soon he would not be in any place long before such requests were made.

He wrote up a pledge to the Collective. From then on all new members agreed, in the name of the Collective, to work for the common good of fishermen, farmers and labourers.

One night Tom sensed that something was not right. It was not so much what was said as how. There was caution in the voices and an indifference in manner towards him that he had not experienced before.

It was not anger. That is a big emotion and by then he was confident enough in both delivery and message to stand and speak to that, if that was it, but it was not.

So first chance he had he took one of the old salts to one side. "Listen, Skipper," he said quietly, "what is all this about, eh? I do not feel a bit of warmth from these people and I can tell you that is some strange on this coast."

"The priest," the old fellow said out of the corner of his mouth. "What?"

"The priest," he said again. "Last Sunday. Said to watch out for you, Mr. Vincent, though he did not mention you by name. But we knowed who he was talking about. 'Our help is with the Lord God,' he preached. 'No man alone can bring about a sea change in the spirit of our time,' was exactly one other thing he said and he told us to beware of anyone who comes who is no doctor yet will make a cure. 'Be mindful of your soul's peril if he asks for your pledge to mere men,' he said, 'and not to God.'"

That evening Tom lost the first place since starting out from Herring Neck. Began as usual but soon found himself talking against clergy, which you cannot do in this country. Truth be told, his heart was not in what he said and in the end he apologized for saying it, which he felt was a weak thing to do on his part, to apologize.

He said, "I believe that God had something mighty to do with the shape of my own life." But they were not listening.

There was not enough interest to ask even for a show of hands, so angrily he tramped out of there by himself.

The priest had also soured the next port-of-call, but knowing then the place was already lost Tom started to speak with the confidence of a man who has nothing to lose. For the first time ever, his speech faltered at its peak and he spit out bitterly that he could not see that the Church was doing anything for anyone, and there and then it was decided in his mind that none would witness such weakness on his part again. Henceforth it would be his style against them all, church or state.

But, oh, he left that night feeling hurt and angry and tired.

He had a headache and he thought about nothing but fighting it off. His spirits lifted only when he reached Our Island the following day. There, unexpectedly, he was met like some hero lately returned from war.

5

It was the brightest of winter days when Tom made it to Our Island. When they saw him trudging across the frozen Channel, they carried the evergreen arch down to where he'd make land, and waited there to greet him. George Gill was behind it all. Beneath the arch George and Tom rushed into each other's arms, hugged and laughed and smacked each other on the shoulders.

"You'll have no trouble setting up a council here," George said. "I've seen to it."

Three women on one side of the arch started to sing and Tom was drawn to one of the singing voices as if it was calling and awakening some hitherto unknown part of himself. Instinctively, he turned to the voice, to a young woman in a fine coat and hat of emerald green, tumbling brown hair, brown eyes. Without a thought he took off his hat and walked straight towards her, and was about to speak when he slipped on ice. His feet kicked out, his arms swung wildly, his hat flew out of his hand. He landed heavily on his back, lightly striking the back of his head as well. He lost his breath and for a moment saw double. The song ended in a shriek, and as some in the welcoming crowd moved towards him, Tom turned quickly onto all fours, gasping for air, and, with one hand, waved them back. His other hand clenched his stomach. Finally, when he was able to breathe, he accepted a hand in getting to his feet.

Tom could not get her image or her song out of his mind. In her, it seemed, was manifest all he had ever desired in a woman, as if every burning thought he had caged and controlled during all his years of enforced celibacy on Reach Run Island had come together to effect a sudden undoing.

When Tom asked George about her, George told him that the talk for years was that Madeline Lane would marry Wes Woolfrey, the oldest son of the local merchant. Tom said simply that he did not care, he had to see her again.

He wanted to know all about her, all about the Woolfreys, too. George told him all he knew.

Once a year, but always on a cold and bright Sunday afternoon, the sound of horses' hooves chipping the Channel ice would carry on the wind to the children skating and frolicking on Sandbank Pond. First one child, then another, would stop what they were doing, and raise their hands for silence. Soon all would be listening, mittened hands to their foreheads to shade their eyes against the sun and the sun on the ice — *"There they are! The Woolfreys!"*

Then everyone saw them, then everyone rushed to unstrap the ice-blades from their boots, to run home with the news.

In no time at all everybody on the Island knew the Woolfreys were on their way.

The Woolfreys always came on Sunday afternoons because no one would be at work or in church then, and they expected all those who were healthy to turn out.

In later years the Islanders knew this meant Wes was home. After he'd moved away to set up the business in St. John's, the Woolfreys visited the Island only when he was home.

Most people had nothing to say. They glumly put on their best coats, hats and boots, stepped out of warm kitchens into the winter afternoon, and from all corners of the Island they trudged to the pond. Everybody going the same way, meeting and moving on in silent groups.

The children excited — chasing one another, tumbling in the snow, screaming.

Before long the two hundred or so men and women of Our Island would be standing on the high side of Sandbank Pond solemnly waiting for the Woolfreys. As the sleighs came closer, the rhythmic chip of hooves on ice came louder, and clearer, and soon you could even hear the shake of the horses' tackle. People started to speak to one another.

"That sleigh can certainly travel, eh?"

"Is Sophie with them?"

"Who's that in the fast little one?"

But everyone knew that only Wes would be in the 'fast little one.' He always arrived fifty or a hundred yards ahead of Tobias and Sophie and Young Toby. How good Wes was, some said, to ride ahead like that, making sure the ice was safe for his family, but it was clear he loved to drive the horses and loved the speed, too.

A long way out you'd see Wes angling for the low side of Sandbank Pond, the forty or so feet that separated the freshwater pond from the sea. Then he'd whip the horse, drive it right off the Channel ice into the snow, the collision of horse and sleigh and snow sending the snow flying — then he would pull back hard on the reins, the horse would stand on its hind legs and cry.

On the Pond the children screamed and scattered. On the high bank, the men and women had seen it all before: some shouted — *"Thataboy, Wes!" "Give it to him!"* — others cheered, and when the horse had settled back down to snorting and shaking the pain out of its head, Wes stood to his full slender height, his teeth showing through his short neatly trimmed beard, the exploded snow falling around him. Then he'd make a theatrical little bow.

Before stepping down from his sleigh, he'd look back across the Channel, pretend that the family sleigh was so far behind that he couldn't see them at all. Then he'd pretend surprise, point and open wide both his mouth and eyes as Tobias glided his team of horses and the heavy sleigh to a soft, sedate halt.

Of course Wes's surprise always brought forth a laugh.

Tobias was quick to get down from his sleigh to throw blankets over his horses. Sometimes Wes did; sometimes not.

By now there was all kinds of cheery talk on the banks.

The Islanders stepped crab-wise down the bank onto the pond.

Young Toby, squeezed between his parents all the way across the Channel, now sprang out of the sleigh to find boys his own age.

Sophie sat grandly bundled up, layered in blankets and furs. She did not wish to be approached and so was left alone.

Talk was lively now as Wes set out on his usual round.

The men on Sandbank Pond gravitated towards Tobias who never strayed very far from his sleigh. He was as big a man as Wes was slim, jovial and friendly and spoke loudly so all could hear what he was saying. Wes, on the other hand, despite his crowd-pleasing antics, preferred to speak to people individually, in an almost formal manner.

Tobias had a great heavy beard and wore a tall fur hat and a long fur coat that was the envy of every man on the pond.

Wes went hatless, wore only a thin black overcoat, always looked cold, but when he shook hands he did not shiver.

"Good to see you," he'd say quietly, calling you by name, as if the recall was a memory exercise for him. Then he would look at you, the bitterest would say, as if he were calculating to the cent how much you were in debt to the family businesses. And make no mistake, all the fishermen but one on Our Island owed 'the Woolf,' and would owe him forever as far as they could see.

From under a blanket on the back seat of the sleigh, Tobias would then haul out a hard black leather case with silver hasps.

Ceremoniously he'd lay the case flat on the seat, briskly rub his hands together and snap the case open to reveal, inlaid in red velvet, a set of half-a-dozen cordial glasses, and a decanter filled with an amber or cherry-red liqueur.

Tobias would take out two glasses and the decanter and fill both glasses. He would wait for the noise of the crowd to lessen, and when it was quiet enough, he would speak.

"Where," he would ask, "is my friend Silas Sainsbury?" Or he might ask for Ches Norris or Alex Knee, anybody — it was said that the name he called was of the man deepest in debt to him, and over the years, many fishermen on Our Island had been singled out in this manner.

"Here!" Silas or Ches or Alex or anybody would answer. Then, hat in hand, he would step forward.

Tobias would take one glass and the other he'd hand to the

fisherman. They'd touch glasses and down the drinks. Talk would start up again, then Tobias would motion to others to come share a drink.

It always reminded George of a church service. It was *more* impressive than most church services, he said, and for sure the Woolfreys came to the Island as often as ministers. And while the ministers spoke on and on about the glory of the afterlife, the Woolfreys were people in glory in *this* life.

And while the ministers exhorted the people to see God's great pattern of power working through their lives, the people had, on a day-to-day basis, first to pay homage to the Woolfreys.

No one ever had to go down to tell John Lane that the Woolfreys were on the Island. The children were afraid of him and would not go anyway — if he was drinking, John Lane could be nasty. But, somehow, John always knew.

He and Madeline were always the last to arrive at the Pond.

Madeline's mother was another of those who'd died in child-birth and John, it was said, was never the same after. He began to drink. He changed his grief into total devotion to Madeline. It was his mission to see she had the best life, and the best life as far as he could see was life with the Woolfreys.

He told people that Madeline had been promised to Wes and at first his talk was dismissed, but this changed when, for their own reasons, the Woolfreys, who'd heard what John was saying, did nothing, by word or deed, to discourage his talk.

The summer that Madeline turned twelve or thirteen (George was not sure) John Lane slaved at his fishing, working both early and late, and much of the day in-between, foolishly and dangerously, many said. People told him not to drive himself so, but by fall, he'd managed to come away from the Woolfrey premises with a small sum of money *in hand* — the only person on the Island not owing.

He'd lost weight, looked more broken and sick than ever, but he patted the money in his pocket, and he and Madeline booked passage to St. John's.

The people on Our Island later heard that in St. John's he took

Madeline to the dentist, not to have teeth pulled like the rest, but to have them 'worked on' — no one knew what that meant.

When she returned to the Island her teeth were white, perfect — but to spend good money on teeth that would rot anyway someday — that was seen as wasteful to the extreme.

When there was a teacher to teach, Madeline was sent to the one-room school. After the first *Royal Reader*, after the first year or so, she was the only child in her level. All the others had left to help their families as best they could.

Madeline finished all the *Readers* in nine years and then became the teacher herself. Her particular joys were mathematics and music. She came to be known for her remarkable singing voice.

To George the arrival of the Lanes on Sandbank Pond was almost as remarkable as the arrival of the Woolfreys.

When people saw John Lane coming, they'd look the other way or mutter under their breath to their neighbours.

John walked wildly, ready at any moment, it seemed, to defend himself from attack. In summer he looked overdressed, in winter he looked cold. He often smelled of moonshine. If people spoke to him as he tramped over the banks — and not everyone would speak to him anymore — he would answer only with a grunt.

Madeline followed him.

George remembered that during her first year teaching she came to the Pond wearing a red coat with black trim at the hem, the cuffs and the collar. The buttons were big and black and she wore a high black hat, her brown hair falling about her face in ringlets. She had paid for it all with her own money from teaching and the quality and style of her clothing that day declared that she was now a woman of her own.

John put his hand on her shoulder, then dashed away. He never stayed to speak to anyone, and although he was much ridiculed, none of it descended on Madeline. She was quick to smile and gentle of manner and all of the Island took a personal interest in her. Poor dear, people said, she never knew her mother, and her father loves the 'shine and is too crooked to speak to.

And no one forgot the talk about her and Wes. So she was special, you see, welcomed everywhere on the Island.

On one of his visits to the Pond Wes could not find her because she was home, in bed with a fever.

The next day, Ronald Gray, a Woolfrey manservant, delivered to Miss Madeline a handwritten note, signed by Wes, saying that he had missed her on the Pond and that he hoped she would soon be well.

John showed the note to everyone.

When Wes went to St. John's, some thought that would be the end of it.

But nothing changed.

When Wes and Madeline now met on Sandbank Pond, they embraced and smiled. Madeline held his hands and he always had something to say to make her laugh.

Wes offered his arm, she accepted, and off they went around the pond — once, twice — as much for the crowd as for themselves, George thought, their heads bent close together in secret conversation and then Wes would take Madeline for a ride in the cutter.

And so the afternoon on the Pond would pass.

Tobias stayed close to the sleigh and sipped his liqueur. He laughed, carried on with the men, and over the course of the afternoon, all came to shake his hand, to pay him their respects.

The children were everywhere into the snow, Young Toby among them, as good, as bad, as the rest of them.

The air was filled with chatter and commotion.

Later in the afternoon as the air turned colder, perhaps there'd be a dwigh of snow, or the sky would cloud over, and the people, duty done, would begin to think of their own needs — meals to be cooked, sick visits to be made — so in small numbers they'd begin to drift away.

Wes would return by himself having taken Madeline home. He'd hitch the one-horse to the back of his father's sleigh, and then he'd track down Young Toby who, when found, would be rumpled, soiled and in high spirits. When Toby was in the sleigh, still yelling to the boys, Wes stripped the blankets off the horses and turned the big team around. Now Wes and Sophie and young Toby all waited on Tobias.

Tobias boarded the sleigh when he was ready, gave a single wide wave, and then sat.

As the sleighs pulled away Young Toby would sometimes kneel on the back seat and wave frantically with both arms. None of the others ever gave a backward glance.

Back on the Pond the laughter and talk died soon as the Woolfreys left.

Everyone went home, closed their doors, stayed in all evening.

At the meeting that evening Tom was light on his feet, and light in both speech and manner, too, and giddy in the head with a renewed sense of purpose. He practically charmed the assembled into forming a council. A time, to begin after the meeting, had been planned if the vote went through early enough and Tom made sure all was concluded quickly.

As the first boys and girls and women showed up, tables were brought out and oilcloths put on, the lanterns were dimmed, and a fiddler tuned up. The transformation from union hall to dance hall was being made, when, unbeknownst to Tom, George announced one more bit of union business.

"Ladies and gentlemen!" he shouted. "Ladies and gentlemen! Your attention please."

Eventually he got them all quieted down. "I want to tell you," he said, "that, this evening, the Fishermen's Collective under President Tom Vincent has just now become the largest union ever in the history of Newfoundland!"

A great cheer went up. Smiles and backslapping all around.

Tom saw her the very moment she entered the hall. Across the dance floor, their eyes met for the second time that day.

Someone called her to a table.

Soon the air was thick and moist and the floor bouncing as the fiddle reeled out the music, and still Tom stood and watched her walking, talking, and he knew by the way she lifted and turned her head when she laughed, the way she smiled — even through the rising noise of the rollicking good time that was about to carry everybody away — he sensed her quiet self-assurance, and it was in a very formal way that he approached her and asked her to dance. She declined.

But he would not be discouraged and even as he bowed his head lightly to her, and stepped back, and turned away, his heart pounded from seeing her up close again — her eyes, a strand of hair out of place, the sheen of perspiration on her forehead. He composed and recomposed her features even as he was walking away.

When Tom turned again, she was standing in a circle of women, her back to him. They were laughing and when he saw one woman fling her arms out, he recognized the mimicry of his afternoon mishap. Another of the circle caught his eye, right away reported this to the others, and, under the press of this new embarrassment, they laughed harder, hands to their mouths. The circle grew tighter.

"George!" Tom shouted, looking around.

George swung off the dance floor.

"George," he said quietly, "I'm leaving. I'm tired. And still there's work to be done."

Tom raised his hand when George protested and sent him back to his dance. Tom squeezed his way through the crowd, avoiding the swinging bodies as best he could, and as he moved across the floor, he saw that Madeline had separated from her circle and was coming towards him. Suddenly she was before him.

"Mr. Vincent," she said, "I am sorry — " But a smile she could not fully suppress flickered across her face. She looked up and away to recover herself.

"Madeline," he said, touching her shoulder. Perhaps she did not know that he knew her name.

Just then the music wound up and up to joyful conclusion, and along with everyone else on the dance floor, Tom and Madeline looked to the stage and applauded the musician, who immediately started playing again, but more softly, slowly.

"Never mind about 'sorry' and all that," Tom said. "Dance this slow one just beginning with me and all will be forgiven."

"Yes," she said.

He put one hand on her waist, she put a hand on his shoulder.

He firmly held her other hand in his own, and they danced, as natural a couple as you would ever hope to see. As smoothly around the floor as if together they'd danced for years. It was a surprise to both of them. Madeline pretended to study their steps, and kept her eyes looking to one side as if this were an aid to concentration. For his part, Tom did not take his eyes off her face. He heard the rustle and swish of her skirts as she moved, and although he would never be able to remember what exactly she wore that evening, he would never forget how the light played across her face. In mid-dance Madeline looked back into his eyes and out of the pure delight of their already perfected rhythm, she could not help but smile her pleasure.

It ended too soon. Tom did not let go of her hand, or take his hand from her waist. They stood there for a long moment. While the rest of the floor clapped and shouted, she once again looked away.

Finally, they parted.

"Thank you," she said, almost in a whisper.

"Shall we have another?"

"I'm sure it would be lovely but I cannot."

Tom raised his eyebrows.

"No," Madeline said quietly. "I cannot. It would be unfair both to you and me because I am engaged, and while one dance is but a courtesy, two would signify intention — "

"Engaged?"

Madeline nodded.

"Well, he is a very lucky man, and I am lucky to have danced with you this evening. If I can ever be of assistance to you — "

"Thank you, but I think not — "

"Then perhaps someday you could be of assistance to me."

"That is very doubtful, Mr. Vincent."

Tom shrugged, smiled. "Tom," he said.

"Goodbye . . . Mr. Vincent."

She turned quickly away and stepped into the crowd.

7

*T*om concentrated on getting out this important message: in the coming season, no Collective fisherman should sell fish unless he receive the yet-to-be-determined union price (or better), and he would personally guarantee the union price to the Collective fishermen if they stood united. Then a bit of luck. Word came down the coast of a merchant in Ragged Rocks that might be willing to pay as high as $6.25/quintal.

So Tom made a visit and learned from his man there that merchantman Hounsell was on the verge of bankruptcy.

Hounsell was a balding man with a square scowling face. He looked unwell, with ropey neck muscles and pale, dry skin, and he did not hesitate to tell Tom at the outset that drink had gotten the better of him.

"Not 'shine," he said, dismissing the common drop. "The real whisky, from Canada, and from the Frenchmen sometimes, too."

He cautioned Tom never to go near it. His business was a near ruin because of it. He was desperate. And now the only salvation he could see would be the fish. He would need fish in predictable abundance to ship and sell in order to buy time and to bring in money so as to keep ahead of it all until he could settle accounts to everyone's satisfaction.

In the end Tom said it might be possible for the FC to deliver the fish he needed, if the price was right, and the right price, Tom insisted, was $6.50/quintal, but Hounsell, desperate though he was, was not going for it and stood adamant at $6.35, and that is the price they settled on.

Later George and Tom stopped at Our Island and went down

to Woolfrey's store hoping to arrange a meeting with Tobias Woolfrey.

They happened into the store when, along with a few fishermen and their wives, the Woolfrey family secretary was standing near a door that led out back to a storeroom opening onto Woolfrey wharf.

Tom straightaway asked Mr. Hunt if it would be possible to meet with Tobias. "There are matters the Fishermen's Collective would like to discuss with him," he said.

Mr. Hunt said nothing at all, and then Wesley Woolfrey himself stepped out of the storeroom.

He inclined his head slightly. "Gentlemen," he said.

Though it was only midday Wes was impeccably dressed in a dark three-piece suit, white shirt and blue tie. The white cuffs of his shirt were just showing at his wrists. His hair was neatly trimmed. Tom caught a faint whiff of cologne.

Wes was as tall as Tom, but of a much slighter build. He pulled his shoulders back a little and clasped his hands behind his back.

Tom asked to speak to him privately, but Wes shook his head.

So Tom went ahead right then and there with his case for better fish prices. After speaking to crowds all winter long he spoke to Wes quietly, but insistently, knowledgeably, and persuasively. A crowd gathered. From time to time, Wes glanced nervously at them but in the end he shrugged.

"I understand what you are saying, Mr. Vincent, but there is nothing I can do."

So Tom told him the Collective would sell fish up the coast for a price almost a dollar higher than his best offer.

"An anomaly," Wes said. "It cannot last. And you will have expenses, Mr. Vincent. Transportation costs" — and here he held a finger in the air as if he were a schoolmaster — "but you aspiring businessmen will soon enough learn that you cannot simply jump into these things. Take my word for it, Mr. Vincent, there will be no profit in this venture for you or your men. Now I have important business out back. I suppose you will go ahead with your foolish enterprise regardless of what I say. Well, good luck to you, Mr. Vincent. You will inconvenience me, of course. But that is all it will be in the end, an inconvenience." Then he spoke over the heads of the Union men to the people standing behind them. "You people around here have done business with me for years, and I will not stand in your way if you think you can do better, even if it is only foolishness that someone has put in your heads." He looked directly at Tom, then at the crowd. "But, my friends, let it be known that when you are ready to bring your fish to me, I will buy. The price we are paying this year" — he looked at Tom again — "the price we are paying this year is *still* $5.50/quintal."

The FC sold all its fish to Hounsell.

They hired schooners to make weekly runs and by midsummer Collective fishermen were enjoying a weak prosperity, but prosperity nonetheless.

More men were joining the FC every day.

All proceeded easily and predictably enough until Woolfrey and Lank raised the prices of everything in their stores. That forced Tom to embark on one of the outbound schooners.

From the deck he shouted to George on the wharf, "Come here!" Tom motioned him aboard. "Come here," he repeated. George stepped lightly from wharf to boat and when he was next to Tom, Tom said, "Look in the hold and tell me what you see."

George gave Tom a puzzled look, looked cautiously down into the hold, blinked, and when he looked up, his face was still wearing the same puzzled expression.

"What d'ya see?" Tom asked.

"F-fish?"

"Right!" Tom answered brightly. "Now, make sure you're here to meet us when we get back."

Six days later.

"What d'ya see now?" Tom asked.

"Barrels of ... what? ... flour, molasses, and look! Twine! By God, everyone's waiting for that."

"Right again!" Tom interrupted. "And the FC owns it all. We changed fish to flour. Bought it all wholesale. Our first wholesale venture."

Tom had no trouble selling his farm on Reach Run Island for a fair price. Now, with the profit from this transaction, he had confidence dealing with the banks in the name of the Collective.

The Collective needed a building for their business centre, and by now it was clear that this would have to be on Our Island, already the place from which all current operations of the Collective were running — this through force of no one's will or intention but simply because of the island's centrality, both geographic and, for a long time, commercial.

So George and Tom took a boat one afternoon when the wind was warm and waters easy, and leisurely rowed around the island, checking water depth, studying the shoreline, and the lie of the land about. They soon found a sheltered cove with water of good depth. Tom said it would do if they found nothing better, and they did not. If ever the place had another name, no one knew it. From then on it was Union Cove.

8

Early one winter morning when Harriet Green was eleven years old, she bent down beside the stove for wood. Her nightgown hitched on the handle of a large pot of near-boiling water. Without thinking she tugged on her gown to free it, but tipped the pot over instead.

The water hit the stove in a blast of steam and the hot liquid launched out for Harriet's left hip and thigh then slopped onto her left foot. Later Harriet would remember the first touch of the water on her skin, a tiny pinch, a nip from a small animal. Then the wild thing hooked itself into her flesh as if to rip that flesh from her body.

Screaming, Harriet tried to crazy-hop out of the pain. She tried to claw the thing away from her, but her father was behind her, his arms underneath her armpits. He lifted her clear off the floor and stepped carefully backwards towards the daybed. Harriet kicked and cried, and Sam could feel strength going from her. He knew from this and from what he could see of the red and rising flesh on Harriet's leg that it was more than he could handle alone. By now the boys had rushed in from outside to see what all the commotion was about — they stood wide-eyed.

"*Rodney!*" Sam shouted. "*Blankets towels — fill 'em with snow! Go boy! Mother — take her clothes off! Sean! Down to Union Cove and get Tom Vincent! Run! Fast as you can! Go! GO!*"

The pain swept over Harriet, took her breath. With her mother's help Sam carefully laid her on the daybed, but suddenly life was in her again. She thrashed about and screamed. Sam grabbed her wrists and held her down.

"Now, now, Harriet," he said quietly. "Tom will be here before you know it. For sure he'll know what to do."

It was just light when Sean led Tom up to the house.

Light shone in every window. They passed Rodney on his hands and knees scraping snow into a red blanket.

"How's Sis?" Sean asked.

"Not crying or screaming any more," Rodney answered, not sure if this was a good or bad sign. His speech did not keep him from his work.

In the kitchen the floor was covered in water.

Harriet was lying half-on, half-off, the daybed. Her head resting in her mother's lap, her mother patting her forehead with a damp cloth. Although her face was beaded with sweat, Harriet looked blue and cold. She was shivering even though a warm dry blanket was wrapped tightly around her arms and body, as much for restraint as for warmth. She was on the edge of the daybed, as if through trial and error the least painful balance point had been found. Her right leg was bent at the knee, her foot flat on the daybed. Her left leg was straight out in front of her, unnaturally at a right angle to her body, heel resting on the floor. Towels covered her loins, to ensure her modesty, and a soaking wet blanket draped her left hip and leg. Sam sat on the floor in front of his daughter; he had a firm grip on her left ankle. He would not let the leg move, and having found a place to grip her leg that did not cause her to scream with pain, he would not let go.

"It's blistering something awful!" the mother said.

Harriet moaned, closed her eyes half in pain, half in grief.

From his position on the floor, Sam looked up at Tom and said quietly, "I fear she'll wear the scald all her life."

Tom knelt in front of Harriet, waited for her to open her eyes. When she did, he smiled, laid the back of his hand on her cheek, rested the palm of his hand there for a moment. His hand was relaxed, dry and warm.

"You're in much pain," Tom said.

She whispered, "Not so much now."

"That's good," Tom said, still smiling. "I am only a farmer, and sometimes a poor fisherman, but, Harriet, what I can, I will do. Do you believe me, Harriet?"

She gave him a single nod.

Tom stood, took off his hat and coat, rolled up his shirt sleeves.

With a small motion of his head Tom ordered Sam to lift the blanket. Very gently Sam released Harriet's ankle and raised a corner, cautiously. Harriet tensed, squeezed her eyes together, and her mother cooed quietly into her ear, soothing her. But as the red-hot and risen flesh was exposed, Harriet whimpered, and as even more of the burn was uncovered, her face compressed with pain and tears streamed from the corners of her eyes. She shivered and shook and might easily have shaken free of her mother had not Tom motioned for Sam to drop the blanket back in place.

Everyone breathed easier then.

Tom lifted the blanket off the thigh that had first met the scalding water — it was one virulently red blister. Tom winced as he looked at it, then laid the blanket back in place.

Rodney stood in the center of the kitchen holding a blanket filled with melting snow. Tom nodded towards Harriet, and Rodney spread the blanket over Harriet's leg and thigh, on top of the blanket already there.

"We were thinking it'd be good to lance that blister," Sam said in a low voice.

"No," Tom said just as quietly, "I don't think so."

"Why not?" Sam asked.

"I don't know," Tom answered, distracted. He was looking around the room, searching. "Can I look in your pantry?"

Sam pointed the way. "Take whatever you need — what do you need?"

"Not sure."

He came out carrying a bowl of eggs. He looked thoughtfully down at them for a moment, then he looked up and said, "I will need all the eggs you can get. Here's what we have to do."

He ordered the boys to keep him supplied with fresh melting snow. He asked Harriet's mother to separate the yolks from the egg-whites and then he mixed the egg-whites and snow into a cool thick solution. As Sam exposed two or three square inches of blistering flesh, Tom dipped his fingers into his concoction and let it drain on the exposed area.

At first Harriet startled when the liquid touched her skin but its coolness was a relief. She quickly got used to the working rhythm of those ministering to her.

Tom spread the liquid to make sure all Harriet's tender flesh was covered. As he applied the balm, he took care not to touch her skin at all because the slightest skin-to-skin contact caused terrible pain.

When each tiny patch had been treated, it was left uncovered and Sam Green lifted the blanket from another small area and the treatment was repeated, over and over.

For most of the morning they worked in silence. The only sound was the cracking of eggshells.

By mid-morning, with most of her hip and legs anointed, Harriet fell asleep and soon all the affected flesh had been covered.

As the liquid dried, it turned opaque and left a white crusty residue.

Tom stood up then. He said that the blisters were not to be lanced and that the white crust should not be washed away — it would, he told them, scale away in its own good time.

And in its own good time it did, and except for a faint red line that Harriet called 'Tom's thigh-water mark,' she did not scar.

PART III

Madeline did not spend time thinking about Tom, but she did not forget him either.

The Woolfreys had a small pleasure boat, a gasoline-motored craft that could sleep just two or three forward, but what it lacked in size, it well made up in speed and quality. The *WW* was known for its immaculately shining hardwood deck and polished brass fittings throughout.

In this boat Wes started to come calling on Madeline. He would come to collect her dressed more for a formal dinner than a boat ride, but his clothes did nothing to hamper his agility. He would cut the engine, letting yacht and tender slowly glide towards John Lane's stage head, and with the efficiency of a practised piece would move from wheel to bow, grab a line, then spring from bulwark to wharf and tie on in a flourish.

Sometimes right away, sometimes after a cup of tea with John and Madeline, but always with John's blessing, with patience and care and smiling elegance, Wes would help Madeline safely down from wharf to boat. Leaving John waving from the stage head, they would set off for the Outer Islands.

These were a chain of tiny islands, low and treeless but thick with blueberry and bakeapple bushes. Pleasant enough on a summer's day, the sun high and warm and the waves gently falling and drawing, but in winter utterly unprotected from the North Atlantic, and bitterly uninhabitable. Here and there you might find a gaze of rocks for a shot at birds, but that was all.

Off one of the islands, Wes would moor the *WW* and row Madeline and himself to shore in the tender. He always brought along a portable easel, small pots of paint, brushes and a small canvas or two, and a large, fully provisioned picnic basket.

He was not particular about where he set up his easel or where they enjoyed their picnic. As soon as they chose a place, off would fly his jacket, then shirt collar and cuffs. He would twist his head to one side as he unbuttoned the top button of his shirt, and then he would smile at Madeline as if, at last, he were free.

When they first visited the Outer Islands, Wes said he would paint her portrait, an informal portrait, he said, with sea and sky and perhaps a little of the island as background. She was so thrilled by the prospect that she found it an effort to be still that first time, an effort to keep from smiling. After maybe half an hour — it felt like two — they took a break. She ran to look at the picture and was disappointed to see that the island, the sea and the sky had been roughed in and painted in fine detail in patches, but she was nowhere to be seen. There was a vague irregular whiteness in the centre of the canvas and she guessed that was her space.

"We'll finish it another day," he said.

But the next time he complained of the changed light all the while he worked. On that day he filled in sea and sky and island, and the colours encroached on the great white space, the space still only suggestive of a shape.

"I'm getting tired of sitting for nothing — paint *me* next time," Madeline pouted playfully.

So he had to try.

But neither could say they were taken with the result.

"Oh," Madeline said. "But I'm not wearing a hat."

"That's not a hat," Wes said.

"Oh."

"It's this light, I think."

"I'm sure you're right," Madeline said. She added, "The light is good for sea pictures, for cloud . . ."

Wes nodded, "I guess."

"Well then," Madeline said brightly, "enough of me sitting around for portraiture — *you* paint, *I* will pick blueberries for later. Agreed?"

"Agreed." Wes nodded, smiled. "Agreed."

She found a jar in the picnic basket and set off. There were berries close by, and soon enough she had almost filled the jar. She straightened up, perhaps to wave to Wes, but ended up watching him instead. The now-abandoned portrait was still on the easel. Wes was staring at it, not moving, then suddenly he swung at the canvas, and knocked it to the ground. He glared at it for a moment. Madeline was not at first sure what had happened, but then she knew. Even from this distance he looked angry enough to put his foot through the canvas. But he did not. He ran a hand through his hair and turned to fitting a new canvas on his easel.

That was private, Madeline thought, not meant for her to see. Best to wait a while before going back. She decided to explore this island a little more.

These explorations became the parts of her trips to the Outer Islands that she loved the best.

She would leave Wes to his painting, take a glassen jar or a cookie tin and walk up over the rise to pick berries. The first few trips, she had not dressed for walking and picking berries. She'd worn skirts and pretty shoes. After that, she brought along trousers. Wes had rubber boots in the boat that fit nicely.

Before she'd walked very far she'd feel as if alone on the island. At first she would be intent at her berry-picking, taking whatever the islands afforded, whatever was in season — blueberries, bakeapples, and, once, small but surprisingly sweet wild strawberries. In no time at all she would fill tin or jar, enough for two. She would feel good about her own contribution to what had already been stuffed into the picnic basket — sliced meats and bread and cheeses and cookies and cakes and jams and jellies and spreads of all sorts, and bottles of fresh water — all tied neatly in an immaculately white linen cloth on which all would be later laid out. Wes had brought it all from Woolfrey House, where, Madeline was sure, it had been made up especially for him.

But now alone, she would stroll down to the beach and shake her hair out and let the sea winds blow through it. She would close her eyes and let the sun warm her face in the moments the sea breezes died down, and she would feel not alone but free. She would take deep breaths of the sea air, letting it out slowly, and a peace would come over her. She was content then to sit on the beach, or to lie back with her hands laced behind her head, to spend time with her thoughts. When she was first free and peaceful like this, her thoughts had come to her all at once, in a rush, higgledy-piggledy, with no rhyme or reason at all, but in time she discovered a shape, a pattern — a helpful way to organize her thoughts about herself and her life and her situation. In one of the *Royal Readers* from which she taught at school, there was a diagram of concentric circles, and she could imagine herself as the innermost circle. For a time she'd been trapped there in the centre by all that was outside of her.

Closest to the centre would be her father — he was the first person, and perhaps the most difficult of all to deal with, for she both loved and hated him. Loved him because he loved her fully and unselfishly. As far back as she could remember she could recall how he would place his hand on her shoulder, sometimes the smell of 'shine on his breath, and, smiling as with some secret knowledge, would look into her eyes, searching deep and seeing what no one else could see, a future, a destiny, undreamt of wealth. When she looked in the mirror and deep into her own young eyes, she tried to see what he saw but could not. You're the special one, he would tell her. Only the best for you, he would say, with no uncertainty in his voice at all. But Madeline had doubts.

She hated him because he drank, and when he drank he was absorbed in the can o' 'shine, and himself, and he talked softly to himself, and wept softly and continuously to himself, and if on occasion she caught his attention, he would stare at her with bloodshot eyes. He would reach out for her, but she would not venture close, and he would slur and burble unintelligible gibberish at her, then look away, as if by so speaking and doing he had set all in order. She could not sleep for his whining and crying and though she hated it when he drank, she always ended up hoping that he would drink more and faster so he would pass out sooner.

One time he fell from the chair, scraped his forehead on the table and hit the floor with a crack. Blood was suddenly everywhere, on her hands, on her night dress, over his face. She made sure he was breathing, then cleaned and bandaged his wounds. She nervously watched over him all night. In the morning he was fine.

And she loved him because she knew it could be worse. When she was young and in school, what was happening to some of her friends at the hands of their caretakers was no secret. Young boys brutally beaten time and again until they were strong enough to fight back, when they were taken out of school and sent to work. Young girls made pregnant by no-one-would-say-who and taken out of school for good.

And she hated him because when she saw him at his work, absorbed completely in his work, she could see the man he used to be. She loved that man, and was drawn to him helplessly. But every time she went to him and touched his arm or called his name, she startled him and he turned and stared at her blankly for a moment as if called back from somewhere distant. There would be a moment of recognition, a moment of reality, and then, always, a look of pain as he remembered where he was, and she hated him for that look. Then he would put his hand on her shoulder, and tell her in that urgent voice of her great future.

Madeline would take a deep, deep breath of salty sea air, exhale it all, a sea change in her thinking.

When they were both very young she and Wes had met for the first time on Sandbank Pond, as naturally and as easily as a drift of destiny. They had later been guided towards one another, but they had found each other first and Madeline wanted to believe that it was meant to be.

About the time she finished school and became the teacher, Wes went to study and work in St. John's. She hardly thought about him at all, but when he came back for a visit and called on her, she was relieved somehow, and glad to see him. When he left again, she was more troubled by his absence. She had responsibilities, was widely regarded as being capable and independent. Everyone came to her to get their letters written and their contracts drawn up and signed and witnessed. She had developed a new maturity, an awareness of the world outside herself and her father. And physically she had become a woman. When Wes had visited she saw him, for the first time, as a man, and that had changed everything. When he returned to St. John's, she realized their oneness had not been unchangeably written in the stars, and she wondered for the first time whether or not he would ever be back, wondered if the future she'd been promised with him would ever come to pass or whether it was just a foolish fiction, and she was suddenly frightened because she now knew what she wanted, and what she wanted more than anything else was to be free, free from all that had been.

Summer came, and as she stepped out to close the door on the last day of school, Wes was waiting for her at the bottom of the stairs, one hand lightly on the rail, the other on his hip, and one foot on the first step. He was smiling, his hair neatly parted and combed, his eyes bright, his suit clean and new.

Her hand went to her mouth, then she ran down the steps, threw her arms around his neck, kissed him quickly on the lips — once, twice — and he kissed back, the full length of their bodies pressing together. Reluctantly they separated and stood apart from one another, smiling and looking at each other in a new way. Even now, the memory of that moment could make her smile.

But out on the barrens of the Outer Islands, berry-picking or walking the beaches by herself, alone with her thoughts, she felt relieved to be free of her father's eye and his obsessions about her. She felt far removed from her responsibilities as a school teacher, far from the expectations and interests of the people of Our Island. She knew even as she thought this thought that all the Island would know by now that she and Wes had once again gone off on the yacht, though no one ever spoke to her about it.

She wondered what they might say if they knew all that happened. Perhaps they did, she thought, or suspected — but she did not care.

On one of their visits to the Outer Islands in midsummer, all had gone as pleasantly as before. The sky was high and blue and cloudless and the sun bright and gracious to all things. But there was a wind, a stiff wind, and a chop in the water. Wes quickly moored the yacht and soon they were in the tender on their way to the beach. They were about halfway when the flat-bottomed boat lifted a little on the chop, then slapped down so that neither of them could avoid the sea spray. It was almost playful.

Though he tried, there was too much wind for Wes to set up his canvas. They soon realized the constant wind would not allow them to picnic in peace.

"We'll take our basket back to the boat," Wes had said, "and enjoy it there." He insisted, however, that Madeline should take her walk, as usual, if she wanted to, if she did not mind the wind. He would be happy to accompany her, of course, but he would be just as happy to wait for her where he was, whatever she wanted.

"I'll pick just a few berries today," she said. "I won't be long." So she set off.

After she'd been gone for . . . she did not really know how long (lost in her thoughts again), she stood up from her berry-picking and the wind struck against her stronger than before. Bearing down upon the island from the north was a low dark squall.

She turned around right away and started back towards Wes and the boat. She thought she heard thunder, deep and low, and she walked faster, or tried to, but the barrens were soft and springy, unreliable, and she stumbled, not falling, but spilling most of the berries from her jar. "Oh no!" she said under her breath, and felt her eyes fill. She took a quick glance over her shoulder and the dark bank seemed dangerously closer. She tried to watch now where she was stepping in order to hurry but her mind was a step or two behind her feet and her fear, so her forward motion (she thought clearly somewhere in her head) was both clumsy and comical and then, looking ahead, she saw Wes urgently waving his arm, waving her towards him, and she ran faster but stumbled again, the rest of the berries flying. She managed not to fall, but had to slow down, for she was out of breath, and now she was close enough to see that Wes was smiling and relaxed as he waited. The urgency had all been in her own mind. She glanced over her shoulder, the darkness almost upon them, her face buffeted by the cold wind.

"Hurry," Wes called, "or we'll get wet."

And they did, they got drenched.

Halfway between beach and yacht in the little tender, the water now black and choppy and resistant, Wes was rowing hard, when drops of rain, thick as the top of a thumb *thupped!* into the boat and in the water around. There was a long hushing sound, then a relentless onslaught of cold, driven rain.

They were soaked in an instant, and just as quickly water was sloshing about in the bottom of the boat. Madeline looked at Wes, the rain a veil between them now, and he smiled. His clothes were plastered to his body, his hair to his head, and great drops of water fell continuously from the tip of his nose. "Not to worry, Maddy!" he called to her over the hiss of the rain. He bent forward, dipped the oars, pulled with a great effort. "Not to worry," he said again, looking over his shoulder, checking the position of the yacht. It was tossing about.

On board, the cold rain drifted across the deck. Just as Wes closed the companionway hatch, there was a flash of lightning, a rip of thunder.

"It's just a squall," Wes said. "It'll pass over in no time."

For a moment they stood facing each other, water pooling at their feet.

Madeline shivered.

"I have towels and blankets and dry clothes," Wes said.

Madeline nodded. Then, not moving from where they were standing, but not looking at one another, they started unbuttoning and peeling off their wet clothes piece by piece.

Neither spoke. Rain and a lightning flash. Thunder and more rain.

They were both naked then, their bodies wet and shining and Madeline shivered again. She crossed her arms across her breasts and looked at Wes. He put his arms around her shoulders and she pressed close. Her arms went round his waist, and they kissed. The boat lurched a little, threw them a little off balance and together they shuffled towards the settee where their kiss was broken and Madeline half sat and half reclined, Wes's knee between her legs. She found a comfortable position and met him strongly as he inhaled sharply. She closed her eyes and bit the inside of her cheek against a momentary sharp pain and she was thinking — some part of her mind always observing, always thinking — that he knew what he was doing, that he must have learned things in St. John's. Where her own response came from she hardly knew. At some point they heard the rush of rain change to a heavy tickety-tick of hailstones.

After that, lovemaking became a regular part of their boat rides, and what had started well got better. Before long Madeline knew she would marry Wes if he asked her, and she knew that he would. When he did, all her anxieties, all her pain and trouble, were suddenly gone.

But she would not forget that after her first time, bare-footed and wearing only one of Wes's shirts which barely covered her, she had opened the hatch, stepped up and looked about. The dark bank was rolling on to the south, the sun beamed down again, and the air was cool and freshened. She had stepped carefully out of the cabin onto the deck and felt the cold pebbled hailstones under her feet, felt their cold lessening as they melted. The wind had died and the water was a deep blue. She had looked up, squinted her eyes against the sun, and to her, unbidden, came the memory of her singular dance with Tom Vincent.

In Union Cove the FC began to build whatever it needed, its pattern of growth determined mainly by merchantmen: that is to say, whatever merchants denied, the Collective supplied.

First came the General Store, the largest on the coast with the offices of the FC right there on the second floor. When they needed their own boats, the reputable boat-building Blackmores of Bonavista North were persuaded to join up, and to house them the FC built a dozen homes. Then, at first independent of the FC, came a woodworking shop, a forge, a machine shop, a bakery and a cooperage, but eventually the Collective owned or controlled them all.

Later, as Collective businesses boomed, they built large fish stores, then more houses. To attract the best men to the various businesses, Tom introduced electricity and the Collective's homes became the first in the country with electric light and electric heat, about eight hours free service per day in the beginning.

When he first brought the electrical experts in to light a few houses, Tom thought of electricity as a novelty. But the contractors soon opened his eyes to its potential, and he opened theirs to practical realizations. He built his own generating station, had all the Collective's industries wired, then conceived of and built the world's first electric fish drier. It covered 20,000 square feet, was fully equipped with electric fans and heaters and blowers, and produced Export Grade fish in less than a day.

The electricians wanted to stay for the good money and working conditions and all that, so Tom hired them on to run the power station permanently.

They electrified the house Tom was building for himself and, so he said, future leaders of the FC. They installed, for his personal use, a master switch for the generating station. When the power was off, he could throw the switch and transform the Cove into a crescent of light for the pleasure of distinguished guests.

Though voices cautioned against quick growth and hasty progress, Tom silenced them by listing the FC's early successes, the best and only argument necessary, he said, against their timidity.

Tom had spent some time walking around the cove trying to find the perfect place for his house. George found him one afternoon standing on a sloping meadow above the cove, looking out to sea.

"See there," Tom said, pointing. "There's a chop of water and crosswind there — do you see that, George?"

"Nope."

"Look closely — *see!* — see that swirl, that turn of the water?"

"No."

"George, are you blind? Stand close. Now look down my finger — straight as if you were sighting down a gun, see that disturbance there? You must."

George shook his head. Try as he might, he could not see the patch of disturbed water that held Tom's attention so.

But on the very spot where they stood that day, Tom later set the cornerstone of his house.

When the St. John's newspapers began to campaign against the Fishermen's Collective, Tom brought a small printing press to Union Cove and the FC began to publish its own sheet of news. It was distributed free to all FC members. Tom's intention was simply to create a forum where he could answer the charges levelled against the Collective in other newspapers, so he called it *The FC Rejoinder*.

Then, because the sheet was in the hands of so many fishermen, some merchant firms asked the Collective for advertising space, and the single sheet doubled, and doubled again to four pages. Soon it was being published weekly.

. . .

People of different faiths were moving to Union Cove and asking for places of worship. Since their numbers were small, they all joined together to design a great church to serve them all alike. All hands threw themselves into this project with Christian zeal and built the edifice entire one Saturday — on FC land and with all materials donated by the FC.

But the building was never consecrated because no priest or minister ever chose to visit Union Cove. Some grumbled this was Tom's fault, that he didn't want it. If he had, they said, he would have found someone to perform the ceremony.

Before long it was boarded up, and boarded up it remained until the night it burnt to the ground.

Across the cove opposite the church, the Great Hall rose up. Built as a place for the congress of fishermen, it was a hive of Union activity and seemed always to be the scene of some robust celebration or other.

On another day George found Tom looking across the channel to the mainland.

"We need ferry service from here to there," Tom said, waving at the distance between shores.

"What for?" George asked. "To ferry what? Sure there's nothing there. People carry over whatever they need in their boats."

"True. But we will need a ferry to transport the bigger shipments the trains will bring us."

"Trains? Sure the nearest train runs miles from there."

"That's why we'll need the spur line. To end at that slab of rock where the rock falls away and the water is deep — then the ferry can come across, round the point there. We can build the receiving depot anywhere in the cove. What do you think?"

George stood looking, imagining the ferry. "Will the others go for it?"

Tom shrugged. "Once we have the spur line and ferry service, we'll have done it. We'll have sea routes, land routes and a place to call our own. We'll be solid. Nothing'll stop us then."

3

On his way back to the cove one night, George took a breather atop a small hill. The moon was high and the sky light. A few dark and ragged clouds ran before the wind at higher levels, but the sea below was smooth and quiet. Union Cove was just beyond the next rise.

The path he now continued on led down from that rise through a grove of tall thin birch, then out into the shadow of the boarded-up church. There, near the narrow side door, a short pale piece of two-by-four lay across the trail. He could easily have stepped over it, but the very sight of it, the simple fact of its not belonging there, brought him to a halt. He sized it up, poked at it with the toe of his boot, then turned it over, the other side showing up as pale as the first. Thinking it very strange, he looked all around, and the only thing he noticed was the door open just a few inches. The length of two-by-four, he realized then, used to bar the door, two six-inch nails in each end. There were nail holes, but no nails in the wood now. He picked it up like a club and walked towards the door until he was close enough to extend his arm and use the tip to open it a little further. The door swung wide, without a sound; George took a step back. Nothing but dark could be made out inside. His first thought had been that some wild animal, a bear, perhaps (though he had never heard of bears on the island), had torn the two-by-four away, perhaps wandered inside. Moving closer to the door, he saw that this was not likely. There were no animal marks at all. Not on the ground, not on the door. The two-by-four had been taken off cleanly and the nails drawn out. By human hands. He wished he had a lantern, but stepped very cautiously into the dark anyway, club at the ready.

"Hello," he said quietly. Nothing. Again, a little louder, "Hello."

They fell on him all at once. He heard a general rustling, something, sack or hood, was yanked down over his head and the tie-cord tightened — burned — around his throat. It cut off any sound he might have made. He tried to give the two-by-four a mighty swing but strong arms encircled and immobilized his own arms, the two-by-four was whipped out of his hand quickasthat, and before he could kick, they had him by the ankles, lifted him clean off the floor. Only a moment — a fraction of a moment — had passed. Inside the hood it was already fearsomely close and humid, but he could breathe until a hand fully covered his mouth and nose. Someone punched him in the arm with such ferocity that it brought tears to his eyes. Had he been able to cry out, it would have been long and loud.

"*Stop yer fightin' and no harm will come ta ye!*" a horrid voice commanded. George stopped, willingly, not so much because he feared he might be harmed, but because he realized it was futile to fight back. "*Good!*" the voice said. "*Make no sound...*" George nodded. The hand came away from mouth and nose, George gulped air, but made no other noise. "*Good! Now stand on yer own two feet and come with us.*" George nodded again, and it came to him that the voice was speaking on the in-breath, in the fashion of a mummer.

Still holding his arms they quickly led him straight ahead, then to the right, then up a flight of stairs. Their footsteps echoed slightly. A chair scraped the floor as it was moved. They stopped, sat him down, let go of his arms. The hood was loosened, then lifted from his head.

At first he kept his eyes closed and let his head fall back. The cool air on his face was a relief, and in his lungs too. His face and head and hair were drenched with sweat. He wiped his brow with his right sleeve. His left arm was too painful to move.

He lowered his head and opened his eyes. He was still in almost total darkness. A small candle, six or seven feet away on the floor, threw a weak and fluttery light. He glanced quickly about and had a vague sense, rather than sight, of men all around.

No one said anything. George looked around again, more slowly this time. Now he could see puzzling shapes and curious forms standing out from the darkness. They not only spoke like mummers but were dressed as mummers as well. Oversized caps and women's fancy hats covered their heads, rags and scarves hid faces. Some had shirts or pants on backwards, others concealed themselves beneath torn dresses or long underwear, and sometimes both, all worn over regular clothes. One of them had a shiny shoe on one foot, a battered boot on the other.

"What have we here, lads?" he ventured to ask. His voice seemed to escape into a great emptiness above his head, and he was as surprised by that as by how steady it sounded, given what had just happened.

Came the calm reply from beyond the flickering candle, "We'll ask the questions, George, if there are questions to be asked." This voice flat and unemotive, but just as hard to recognize or place as a mummered voice.

George looked to where the voice had originated, somewhere beyond the small half-sphere of candlelight, but he could see nothing.

Nobody spoke for a time. It was very quiet. George stretched his legs out, crossed his feet, slouched in the chair. He thought about crossing his arms, but knew that would be too painful, so he rammed his hands into his pockets. He looked around again, sneered at them all. The very picture of defiance, he waited, expecting at any moment to be knocked off the chair and beaten again. And he was ready for that. They would not surprise him this time. He was ready to fly with mighty rage if they came at him again, and he rather hoped they would. But they did not. Nobody spoke for a time.

The flat voice asked then, "How goes the work on the President's bungalow?"

George snorted. "You brought me here to ask me that? That's plain for all to see."

"He's moved into one of the finished rooms," said the voice, as if George hadn't spoken at all, "and the house continues to grow up around him every day. A serving girl has moved in. Perhaps you can tell us what she's serving." There was a meaningful pause. "Perhaps we can get a little of it."

Snickering all round then. And George right away knew what they were getting on about, but could not guess how they knew. Surely the girl would not tell. By accident he had discovered her in Tom's room one morning, but had spoken to no one about it, not even Tom, for Tom was asleep. But dark-haired Alice stood naked before a mirror, having only just risen from the bed. George was in the doorway seconds only, but in his mind it seemed he stood there a long time. His jaw must have dropped to his boots, he guessed, and it took him a long time to *understand* the nakedness, and longer still to believe, and it seemed to take forever for Alice to turn her head towards him. She made only the pretence of an effort to cover herself. After seeing all there was to see of her, his eyes ended up looking into hers. She raised a finger to her lips and shushed him, and he stepped back, pulling the door closed.

Only Alice could have told them.

"Or a taste of his liquor at least?" the voice said.

"Look," George said impatiently, "what in hell's flames do you fellers *want*? Tom works harder than any two or three of you put together, of that I'm damn sure, so who the hell are you to throw up dirt about his women, and what odds if he takes a drink or two?"

"Oh," came the soft reply, "we'll not deny any man his pleasures — not his house or his women or his whisky. Oh no, not at all. But we do believe, just as Mr. Vincent says he does, that we all deserve a fair share, and that we should have a fair *say* in how it is shared."

"And do you not?"

"Hmmph! Are ye daft man? Do you not pay attention at meetings?"

George shrugged, hands out of his pockets showing empty palms. "What?" he said. "A meeting is a meeting — same as always."

"Exactly," came the quick reply. "No matter how many voices we raise against him on anything, he does not hear."

"*I'm* not the one who's daft here," George interrupted. "How can you say he does not hear? Look at all he's done for all of us, and you all bloody well know it, too. None of us have ever had it so good. That's why you have to all go sneaking around at night and meeting in secret because you know your accusing could not stand up to the light of day. Not a soul would be listening to you, and no one believing even if they did listen — "

The voice came back, calm, but not as calm as before, "There's big money coming in, George Gill, and no accounting on how it's going out. And hardly any of it goes out on anything other than what *he* wants. Whatever he wants. *His* projects — the spur line for the train, the ferry and the ferry dock — whatever he wants, no matter that we don't need it, no matter the expense, no matter how many of us speak against it. The whole bloody ferry thing is folly, a point of pride for him — we should stay the course, stick to what we know, and what we know we can afford — "

"And *you* know better?"

"*All* will suffer otherwise, and you know that as well as any of us. There's worry in your voice, too, when you've spoken up on these matters. And he's told you to be quiet."

Which was true, and George knew then that some of these conspirators were highly placed, close to Tom and himself, members of the innermost circle, participants in their most heated disputes, who were now taking their cause a step beyond.

The voice: "We have our own visions, George. But *he* does not see, does not bother about them. His own vision has become our tyrant. He is letting the common day-to-day things go, he has forgotten already where we have come from and what we were built on. He — *we* — will lose it all if we are not careful."

"Take it up with him then, open-faced, like men, not cowardly like this."

"He does not listen. He does what he wants, *only* what he wants."

Between clenched teeth George hissed, "He has done nothing wrong."

He was answered with a long silence. The candle flared, seemed about to go out, but did not.

George heaved a heavy sigh. "What do you want from me?" he asked almost petulantly.

"A collective needs a collective vision, not a singular one. Before long, like it or not, there are going to be changes here, George, and it would be best for all concerned if it were done smoothly. You're for us or against us, George — no, don't answer now. We know what your answer would be if you answered now, after being treated so harshly, and after we slandered your good friend. So take some time to think on it. I was saying it would be best for all if the changes are made without too much fuss. You know Tom better than any of us. He confides in you what he would confide in no one else — perhaps at a certain time he might share some confidence that we might have need of."

"Never! Never will I spy!"

"Perhaps we'll only need your support in an important vote. We must know, though, that come what may, we can count on you."

"No!"

"You'll need time to think it over for sure. And think about this: change will come, peaceful . . . or otherwise. Which it is makes no difference to us, but you may want to protect your friend. The less he resists the better for us, the better for him."

"Nev — "

"*Quiet!*" came the sharp reply. Then after a moment, calm again. "We're done for now, George." Then a hand quickly pinched out the candle flame plunging all back into the deeper dark. The voice said, "Best for you to keep your own counsel on this. The less Tom knows, the better. We'll know what you're doing. We'll let you know when and where we'll want to meet with you again. You will come. Now, stay just where you are for a few minutes, George."

There was general movement, a rustle all around him that faded quickly away, in all directions. Footfalls, whispers, then a door slammed, echoed through the empty space like a shot, startled him. Then all was quiet except for the sound of the silence in his ears. He was sweating, he realized, and his arm ached. He waited in the darkness as he'd been instructed to do and tried not to think of anything. He did not want to think on any of it at all. Then he stood up, and because he knew the layout of the church, he easily found his way down from the balcony and back to the side door and stepped out.

The night sky was as light as it had been before, but now the wind that had been at higher levels had come to earth, and breezed through the trees, and felt good on his face.

There was not another soul about.

His left arm pained whenever it moved.

Tom was behind his desk leaning way back in his chair, hands laced behind his head. He said nothing but didn't miss a word. He smiled and raised his eyebrows when George mentioned Alice, but that was all.

When George finished his tale, Tom raised his eyebrows again, shook his head. "Incredible," he said. Then he sat upright, leaned to one side to open a desk drawer, pulled out a half-empty bottle of rye whisky and two glasses. George shook his head and Tom put one of the glasses away. He poured himself a drink and drank it down straightaway, then poured himself another and put the bottle back in the drawer.

Not long ago Tom had surprised George with an offer of whisky to celebrate — what? The start of some new project or other, George could not remember which one. After that it became routine for Tom to be taking a drink or two every day.

Now Tom looked at George, shrugged his shoulders, shook his head, pulled the corners of his mouth down. "I don't know," he said. "I don't understand."

"What is there to understand, Tom? You've got people who are going to be coming against you somehow. They don't like the way you've been doing things."

"But, George, I know these people better than anybody. I brought them here and together we built all of this. They are living better today in this place than anybody like them has ever lived in this country before. They'll not rise up against me."

"Not all of them, Tom, no. But some of them. Some of them have plans — why are you shaking your head?"

"I talk to these people every day. I clean their wounds, pull their teeth. If there was any such talk against me, make no mistake about it, they would tell me. For sure I would know."

"If they knew."

"They would know."

"For sure?"

Tom nodded. He raised his glass to his mouth, wet his lips with the whisky.

George said, "And before you know it we'll be out on our arses wondering what happened to us." He was only half-joking.

Tom smiled. "Do you suppose it might have been a prank?"

George shook his head, rubbed his arm. "It didn't feel like fun," he said.

Tom was watching him closely. "Okay," he said. "If and when they get in touch with you, let me know."

George nodded.

"I don't think you'll hear from them again."

"But," George asked, "isn't there something we could do to be ready, just in case?"

"I think," Tom said, smiling, "any reaction would be *over*-reaction."

Time passed. A week, two. Nothing happened. They talked about it less and less. The pain in George's arm disappeared, and were it not for the shadow of what had once been an ugly bruise on his arm, he might almost have convinced himself that nothing had happened. Even so, with the passing of time he started to come around to Tom's way of thinking that it was all a joke. In his heart of hearts he hoped that was it, but in the same place he knew it was not.

Early one afternoon, after they'd taken a small meal in the kitchen, Tom hurried off to inspect the new extension to the house. He was interested in his house in all its stages and aspects, and he was especially proud of his decision, despite all objections, to live in the house before it was completely finished. There was sawdust and clay everywhere, but he did not care. It made him feel part of it, he said, and it gave him energy somehow.

As Alice was clearing the table, she whispered in George's ear, "Tonight at ten, same place as before."

George looked at her but she was deliberately not looking back. She finished her work quickly and then left, having said not another word. George sat there, his heart pounding in his ears.

Tom's chat with one of the workmen died as George approached. Something — the urgency of his stride, the tension on his face — communicated high seriousness. So Tom hurried to meet him.

"What?"

George told him.

At first Tom looked as if he did not hear, and George was about to tell him again, but Tom shook his head. A puzzled look passed across his face, then profound bewilderment. He opened his mouth as if to speak but no words came. He motioned with his hand, as if about to ask George a question, but still no words came. He looked straight up, exhaled all the air from his lungs, and looked straight back into George's eyes.

"I — They — " He gave it up and looked at his feet. He kept shaking his head, and when he looked up again, tears were welling in his eyes. He blurted out, "I — I'm — struck dumb — struck me dumb!"

He turned to walk away, but stopped, composed himself. "Regardless," he said, "there'll be much to do to ready ourselves for later." Then, slowly, as if afraid, he turned around to look and search in George's eyes.

"Don't even ask the question," George said.

When Tom swung the door open, he had whisky on his breath, and a full glass in his hand. There was a crazy dance in his eye. He threw his head back and downed the whisky in a gulp. He tossed the empty glass to the floor behind him. It bounced once then shattered.

"C'mon," he said. Stuck on his hat, grabbed his coat, slammed the door shut behind them. Already he was in the lead, striding away, even as he worked his arms into his jacket.

Outside it was near dark, everything in silhouette against a slick
of lemon sky in the west.

Tom led the way down a back path and followed a roundabout
route to a storage shed. He lifted the latch and they slipped inside.
The air was sharp with kerosene.

"Just wait," Tom whispered.

Gradually George's eyes adjusted, and he made out the shapes of
the casks. He knew they were blue, but he could not see that in the
dark.

Tom was scurrying confidently about. George heard the clink of
glass on glass.

"Two for me, and two for you!" Tom whispered again. "Come
here, George."

George moved cautiously through the dark towards the voice
and found Tom standing next to two casks, one on top of the other.
A gallon bottle popped hollowly when he uncorked it.

"Hold this here," Tom commanded. George took the bottle and
held it beneath the spigot. The wooden handle squeaked as Tom
turned it. The kerosene spurted out into the bottle, some of it
washing cool over George's hands.

Night was now fully down, and cover enough, but they stood
stock-still behind birch trees and bushes, watching the side door of
the church.

The first of the conspirators, two of them, appeared well before
the appointed hour. They did not speak and it was too dark to
recognize them. They were wearing hats pulled low down on their
brows, and each carried a parcel underarm. They strolled down the
path that passed the side door and if they glanced towards the church
neither Tom nor George could see it. They walked well past the
church and were lost in the darkness. Only a few minutes passed
before they returned, parcels still underarm. This time their stride
was more purposeful and both were turning their heads left and right
and from time to time glancing back over their shoulders. They
examined the side door, the two-by-four nailed across it again. They
ducked out of sight around the corner of the church. When they

reappeared they were in mummer garb, and now they worked fast and furtively. With one of them looking up and down the path, the other went to work on the two-by-four. The only thing Tom and George heard was the groan of one of the nails as it was drawn from the wood. But it was done quickly and the one who'd pried off the two-by-four threw it to his fellow who was very careful about where and how he laid it across the path. When it was just so, he dashed to the side door with his mate. Mummer rags flying, they disappeared into the dark, the door swinging quietly shut behind them.

George could not see Tom's face though he could hear him breathing, short and heavy. Out of the shadowy woods came a shadowy man already dressed in rags. Like every one of the dozen or so that followed, he first checked the two-by-four on the path, looked carefully all around, and then went inside the church. They were all inside before the hour.

Tom murmured something that George could not really hear, but he knew by Tom's small restless rustling movements that he wanted to move.

"You take the bottles," he said to George in a normal voice, then stepped out of cover and walked briskly towards the church. George awkwardly followed, balancing, cradling, four kerosene bottles in his arms, care and caution in every step.

He's going to walk right in on them, George thought. Tom picked up the two-by-four, almost without breaking stride, then stopped to wait for George, and George was sure he knew what would happen next. But when he caught up, breathing hard and damp with sweat, Tom chose not to enter. He'd been leaning on the two-by-four like a cane. He let it fall away from his hand, then took two of the bottles.

"Wait here," he said, and disappeared around the corner. George stood looking about, nervous and feeling rather useless but not knowing what else to do. Uncomfortable out in the open, he moved in closer to the church and felt the better for it.

George was watching the corner where Tom had disappeared, but Tom startled him by coming suddenly up from behind. "Give me another," he said, the kerosene stink on him. He took the bottle and hustled away. George glanced back the way Tom had come, saw a weak glow on the trees, as of a light shining out from the far end of the church. It flickered, brightened. "Damndamndamn," George said, straightening up, his heart pounding, every sense now intensely alert. He heard the *woof!*, saw a sudden illumination at the near end of the church as Tom lit the fire there too. Tom hurried around the corner, looking behind him, then at George. One side of Tom's face was brightly lit, the other in deep shadow.

The first hint of smoke reached his nostrils.

"Now," Tom said, gleefully, "the last one — give it to me!" George was too stunned to hold it out, so Tom grabbed it roughly. He went directly to the side door, swung it open.

Flames just then began to lick at and creep along the eaves.

Tom reached way back with the bottle, flung it through the door. George heard it shatter.

Tom shouted inside, *"All you need to know of power!"* Then, with a quick flick of his thumb, he scraped the thick head of an Old Sea Dog match across the friction strip of the box. It sparked, arced and flared above the spilled kerosene — fumes to flames in a flash, Tom raising his arm to shield his face from the heat.

He slammed the side door shut, loped back over to George and stood there, legs wide apart, arms across his chest, watching.

"It's all dry wood, see," Tom said, "dry as a bone. Good wood, went up like that!" He snapped his fingers. "It won't be long now."

George was speechless.

Smoke was swirling all about them, flames were shooting, now and then, above the peak of the roof, and had taken hold at the corners.

Tom chuckled to himself. Then what he had been waiting for came to pass: the side door banged open and in a dreadful mass, climbing one atop another, the conspirators, still in mummering rags, disgorged. They ran every which way, save one with clothes on fire and frantic because of it and another who stayed to help him tear off his flaming costume. When that was done, they too ran, but towards Tom Vincent and George Gill standing implacable in their way. They stopped running all of a sudden, screamed and cursed then fled away in greater terror.

The fire was further along than George would have guessed for the time that had passed since it had been set. He watched its progress with fascination, but Tom turned his back on the conflagration and walked back into the trees, the way they had come. He was soon lost to sight in the deeper and darker shadows, removed from it all.

Still not having said a word for or against, George took one last look at the conflagration, then followed.

They were not long gone when the first citizens from the cove arrived on the scene, but they were all too late.

A strange time, that next morning. Everyone was shocked and sad that the church could not be saved. Bewildered, too. Everywhere they turned that morning someone was missing. A neighbour or a friend or someone you'd worked alongside, day in, day out, who'd simply up and gone while the fire raged. Some of the missing had been seen leaving, or at least preparing to leave: as most of the cove headed for the smoke and flames, a certain number — a baker and a blacksmith and a boat builder, and now add to the list an electrician and one of the schoonermen and the maid Alice — had been seen moving about, now that people thought back on it, as if attending to personal affairs. They'd taken some small boats, but abandoned most everything else.

Thus ended dissent in the Fishermen's Collective.

And after two weeks of unwavering dedication to the drinking of Canadian Rye Whisky, Tom told George he hoped soon to swear off the booze for good.

PART IV

After it was all straightened away with the merchantman Hounsell, everything ran smooth as clockwork for the rest of that year, and for the best part of the next season.

That second summer Madeline Lane married Wes Woolfrey, a big wedding in St. John's.

"Well," Tom said when he heard, "that ship has sailed." He did not speak of it again but George sensed he was more affected by the news than he let on.

Then one day very late in the fall, as they were about their work on Our Island, someone called out, "Mr. Vincent! Mr. Gill!"

Tom and George stopped mid-stride and turned. A young boy ran up and handed one envelope to Tom and another to George. The boy must not have been able to read because he gave Tom's envelope to George, and George's to Tom. So the envelopes were exchanged. "They're from Mr. Wesley Woolfrey," the boy said. "He told me to wait for an answer."

The names were very carefully handwritten across the envelopes. They pulled out identical cards, stiff and very expensive, with the yellow and black Woolfrey flag emblazoned on the front. Invitations to an evening dinner at Woolfrey House, two days hence. Wes Woolfrey himself had signed.

"Well?" the boy said.

Tom looked at his card, rubbed it quickly and lightly between his thumb and finger.

"We'll think about it," Tom said, and he sent the boy away. They walked on quietly for a little while and though Tom said nothing, George knew he was thinking of Madeline. But when he stopped and spoke, he said, "Something is happening, George. We must go."

Later that day, on plain white paper in a plain white envelope, delivered by their own messenger, they accepted Mr. Woolfrey's invitation.

The entrance to Woolfrey House was brightly lit and shining in the company colours. The door was high and wide and solid-looking. Tom guessed it was made of some kind of heavy imported hardwood naturally flat black in colour. The knocker and the door knob were made of brass, the door casing and sidelight sashes were painted yellow, and against the black ground these brightnesses were striking.

A manservant swung the door open, spoke their names, and welcomed them to Woolfrey House. When they were inside he took their coats and hats and said: "Gentlemen, Mr. Woolfrey and his guests are eager to greet you. When you are ready — this way, please."

They followed him slowly down a long and wide and carpeted hall with a high ceiling intricately sculpted in patterns of fern and flower. Doors on both sides of the hall were open, by design; Woolfrey House was on display for them. With a combination of gas, candle, and lantern lighting, the house was well and evenly lit throughout. All the rooms they saw into that night had walls of highly polished panelled wood. No room was without a fireplace, and no fireplace was without a roaring fire illuminating scenes of foxes and hounds, of shotguns and pheasants, embroidered on the finest of fire screens. In every room expensive furniture was tastefully distributed in exact proportion to the room's size and function. All about were porcelain ornaments, fine lamps, decorative plates, music boxes and elaborate ashtrays, every one a small treasure.

George was taking in all these riches when he bumped into the servant.

"I'm very sorry, sir," the servant said, "but I believe we should wait for Mr. Vincent."

George had quickly glanced over the paintings hung on both sides of the hall but Tom had lagged well behind to study them one by one. So now George, too, took an interest.

To his eye they were good paintings, finely detailed, brightly representing things as they were: the Woolfrey schooners *Hardnose*, *Jam Tack*, and *Knuckle*, Woolfrey House itself, and the Woolfrey Premises on the mainland and Our Island.

Tom noticed what George did not, and pointed out to him, in the bottom right hand corners, the initials *WW*.

"Our host," Tom said.

"Right you are, Mr. Vincent!" Wes Woolfrey said, suddenly standing where his manservant had been.

Tom turned and said without a moment's hesitation, "I would say your work gives a false impression of our climate, Mr. Woolfrey. Our weather is seldom as bright and cheery as it always seems to be in your pictures. Otherwise, I have to say, you are a very good painter indeed."

"Perhaps I was," Wes said, slowly approaching them, "perhaps I was. A good draughtsman, at least." Then after a moment, "But I paint no longer and no longer make any claims at all to artistry. What you see on these walls is the lot, the last and the best."

"But surely," Tom said, "it is dangerous to turn your back on such talents?"

"I think not," Wes said flatly, dismissing the matter. Then, as if remembering his role as gracious host, he added, "I spend no time reflecting on such things. I am what I am; I do what I do, and if there is a peril in what one does *not* do, it has not become evident to me. I thank you for your kind words nevertheless."

They moved away from the pictures then, Tom and Wes walking shoulder to shoulder, until Tom's eye was caught by the model of a low-slung horse-drawn carriage, which stood on its own shelf, at about chest-level.

It was made of pure silver, exquisitely detailed in every respect, from the perfectly tackled horses to the tips of the pennants flying at the ends of lances held aloft by footmen riding the back step of the coach. Atop the roof of the coach, just behind the jolly silver driver, all manner of luggage was stacked and strapped.

"Ah," Wes said, "let me show you this."

He smoothly lifted the lid, which was the roof and luggage all of a piece, and revealed an interior tightly packed with short strips of thick printed cardboard.

Wes said, "When our family dines, the silver coach often provides topics for conversation. Why not take one, Tom, as a souvenir of your visit?"

Tom plucked a strip out at random and read it, Wes looking over one shoulder and George over the other.

> Where there is no vision, the people perish.
> Prov. 29:18

"Indeed," Wes said, raising his eyebrows. "An inspired selection. Mr Gill, would you care to make a choice?"

George declined, so Wes replaced the silver lid, as Tom tucked his souvenir into a jacket pocket.

Although spacious and high-ceilinged, Woolfrey House's splendid dining room seemed warm and comfortable. A huge gas elier, the first Tom or George had ever seen, hung from the centre of the ceiling, flanked by two lesser chandeliers. The room was drenched in light. There was a fireplace, too, with a marble mantelpiece and a small fire, and a great oval table with lovely high-backed chairs, and place settings already laid down, light accenting the silverware. There was a high china cabinet, draperies — all of the very best.

Throughout the room men in small groups talked and laughed and drank from long-stemmed glasses.

Hounsell, the FC's man in Ragged Rocks, was there.

All in the room registered the new arrivals but conversation continued unabated.

George whispered to Tom, "I believe — "

And Tom started, as one sometimes does involuntarily when almost asleep. "I believe," George whispered, "all these men are merchants."

Tom nodded.

"Well," Wes said to Tom, "the route you've taken to get here is somewhat different from the paths my friends here have taken, but it makes no difference how you got here, Mr. Vincent. The important thing is that you are *here!* Come! These are people I'd like you to meet."

So they made a round of the room, and George was right. Merchantmen, every one of them. They exchanged courtesies with Tom and George and eagerly listened to anything the Unionists had to say, but volunteered very little themselves, not that they had much of a chance. After each introduction, Wes quickly moved them on.

Tom and George wanted to speak to Hounsell more than anyone else, of course, but Hounsell kept away from them. He wouldn't look either of them straight in the eye at all, these men he'd been conducting a healthy trade with now for well over a year.

Tom suddenly broke away and strode directly towards Hounsell. George followed, saw Hounsell's eyes go wide as Tom thrust out his hand. Hounsell gave him a nervous laugh, a sweaty hand.

"Good to see you, Hounsell!" Tom said heartily.

Hounsell winced.

"Of course you already know Mr. Hounsell," Wes said, stepping between them. By the elbow he gently turned Tom one way. Hounsell was quick to move in the other.

At that same moment, a servant tinkled a small bell. "When the gentlemen are ready, dinner will be served."

Wes showed Tom and George to seats, Tom at the very end of the table, George to his right. Wes took his place at the opposite end, facing Tom, Hounsell on his right.

For a time the room was crowded with servants, male and female. The elegant arrangements of false flowers that had decorated the table were whisked away and replaced with lit candelabra. Soup tureens and platters were placed, steams and the richest of smells swirling about.

Wes stood, coughed. All went quiet.

"Let us give thanks," he said.

They rose as one and all together bowed their heads. Except Tom, who was watching Wes, and George, watching both of them. Wes spoke clearly, head down, but glancing first to one side then to the other. Then he raised his head and locked eyes with Tom. Thus they remained until the Amen.

After a moment Wes said, "The serving girls are the only women with us this evening. Gentlemen, please, enjoy yourselves."

Everyone sat, and the feast began.

George lifted a knife, impressed by its silver weight and even balance. The service caught Tom's eye. A simple design: plain white, a single blue line around the outer edge and in the north position of each plate, bowl, cup and saucer, the Woolfrey flag. As Tom admired the lightness of the crystal wine glass, a woman's voice spoke quite close to his ear.

"Would you care for wine, sir?"

Tom looked around, found himself staring into the face of one of the serving girls, a bottle wrapped in white linen in one hand, a silver filter in the other.

She had red hair piled high on her head in a loose knot. "Some wine, sir?" she repeated, lifting the bottle.

"No."

"Very good, sir."

Tom could not keep his eyes off the girl, one of several now pouring wine around the table. A bald-headed man with prodigious muttonchops sideburns squeezed her full on a buttock as she bent over.

Tom held his breath, but the girl very calmly brushed the plump hand away, scolding the man with just the tiniest shake of her head — much as you might signal to a child misbehaving in company. The man took some delight in this, and as the girl stepped back from the table, he lifted his wine glass and bowed his head to her, a private toast. She responded to his toast with a little smile, but as soon as he looked away, it was as if a mask fell from her face. Her smile disappeared and her true countenance was revealed: tormented and mysterious.

A moment later the smiling mask reappeared.

. . .

Neither Tom nor George had ever tasted such food. Flaked cod smothered in a thick white sauce which, Wes suggested to one and all, should be sprinkled with slivered almonds. All agreed that it was a unique dish, very tasty. Coming from men who'd eaten cod in most of its preparations, that was a high compliment.

There was lively talk all around, but Tom and George spoke mainly to one another. By the time pudding and hard sauce were put away, both were leaning back, sated and quiet.

Boxes of cigars made the rounds and smoke was soon drifting across the table. The conversation got louder.

The table was cleared, and, as before, they were offered wine, which Tom once again declined with a sad look on his face. He watched the young serving women, efficiently intent on their work, stepping in and out to refill wine glasses and brandy snifters. The men now seemed to be much freer than before, more careless about where they let their hands fly, fall and feel. Buttocks, thighs, a breast. Some exchange at the other end of the table prompted raucous laughter. One of the girls ran from the room.

Wes rose.

Everyone had loosened ties or belts, and several were feeling the wine, but Wes was as composed as he had been before dinner.

"Gentlemen," he said. As if on cue all the serving people filed out. The talk at the table died down.

"Gentlemen, I would like to propose a toast." He lifted a bottle of wine, and, standing very properly straight, one hand behind his back, carefully poured for himself. When the glass was near full, he put the bottle down. He lifted the glass and the wine caught the candlelight, casting a wavering, refracted ring of light around the room.

He said, "To the men who united the fishermen of this coast. To the men who reminded us of *our* duty to one another. To Mr. Tom Vincent and Mr. George Gill!"

To Tom! To George! — it came from all around the table, glasses were lifted and the wine in them disappeared. Tom looked more puzzled than pleased. Wes took a small sip of his wine, set his glass down.

Tom nodded to the table. "Thank you, thank you," he said modestly.

Wes, still standing, smiling, hitched his thumbs into the pockets of his vest. When the room was quiet again, he said, "No, we must thank you, Mr. Vincent."

He paused and Tom shrugged. "I don't understand why," he said. "It seems somehow that we're at odds with one another these days."

"Perhaps we were for a time, Tom. But those days are behind us, or we should put them behind us. We'll speak about that later. But as to how you've been a service to the merchants of this coast, that's really quite simple. We businessmen tend to be independent types. We all know one another but we go our own way, try to make a good living and have as little as possible to do with our . . . competitors." A few of the merchantmen chuckled here. "This is good when the going is good, but when things go wrong," and Wes looked down at Hounsell who was staring at his wine glass, "when things go wrong, there is then no one to help." Wes looked directly at Tom. "You have shown us what can be accomplished when men stand together. We have taken notice and we have been chastised, Mr. Vincent. You and your Collective have been somewhat more of an 'inconvenience' than I ever thought you could be."

There was a smattering of nervous laughter around the table.

Wes smiled, inclined his head in recognition of Tom's accomplishments. "I accept that," Wes said. "It's business, and a good businessman is adaptable."

Wes looked up at the ceiling, his palms showing outward.

"How, I asked myself — we all asked ourselves — how could this have happened here?" He levelled his gaze and looked around the table. "And in the end we discovered we had in part brought it upon ourselves by neglecting our own."

Wes looked at Hounsell again.

"That situation has been corrected."

For the first time that evening, Hounsell voluntarily looked straight at Tom.

"You tricked me," he shouted petulantly down the length of the table. "You took advantage of me when I had troubles!"

Tom looked hard at Hounsell but said nothing.

"All of us about this table," Wes said, "excepting yourself and Mr. Gill, are now in complete agreement on the importance of regular communication between one another, about helping one another out . . . and we are also agreed on a new price for fish. You will now have to go much much further than Ragged Rocks, Mr. Vincent, to get the price you have been getting for your fish. A very long ways indeed.

"Now, Tom, we can appreciate your situation. We know what a fine setup you had, and we're not insensitive to your aspirations. We would not want to see you left out of our own little 'collective.' That is to say, businessman to businessman, we sympathize with your plight. We've all agreed that you will have your fair share, if you join with us. We'll leave it to you to explain and sort it out with your men. I hear you're quite good at that. And there's no need to give us your answer right away. We've plenty of time. Now," Wes continued, a lighter note in his voice, "we've had good food and this has been a good conversation. And there's some frolic yet to come. My wife had to be away this evening but the women, you noticed the women — they were hired for talents additional to their culinary and serving skills."

From all around the table, there were hoots and whistles of approval, as if some tension had just broken. A few men clapped and there were calls to bring them on.

"Restrain yourself, gentlemen," Wes said. "There will be time enough and enough good times for all. Including Mr. Vincent and Mr. Gill, if they so desire. As to the other matter, Mr. Vincent, we ask you to think it over. We're making you an extraordinary offer. One that will not be made again. I am sure you will consider it carefully, very carefully."

Tom was to his feet in an instant. His chair crashed to the floor, but his controlled voice belied his anger.

"I cannot accept your offer, Mr. Woolfrey." He almost sounded amused. He smiled, shook his head. "If I joined up with you, all my work would count for nothing. It would set fishermen right back where they were." He paused. "Or, now that I think about it, further back. Yes, it would set them further back. Because before long, I'm sure, you would all want to reclaim what they've gained, what they've taken from you." Apparently forgetting who was speaking, a few of the merchants nodded. Tom looked at them incredulously. "And more besides, to make up for the trouble they've caused you?" They nodded again.

"You and I both know," Wes interrupted, "that your vision cannot be achieved in this generation."

"So you would condemn us to lives of servitude?"

"And you would sacrifice the present to an uncertain future?"

"It will be a long hard fight to cast off all that needs casting off, but we will for certain recover and restore ourselves to ourselves, in spite of the unnaturalness of the lives you have tried to force us to live."

"It is in your hands then Mr. Vincent."

"Oh, it would be so very easy to be like you, Wes. Many like me have followed those like you before, but now it must be different."

"How, Tom? Will there be violence now?" He paused, raised an eyebrow. "Torchings, perhaps? Or bloodletting? Now that this struggle is ... joined?"

"We can be imaginative, Mr. Woolfrey, as well as organized. Organization is only the bare beginning of it."

"Then go and be damned, Tom Vincent!"

Tom was silent for a moment. He studied Wes Woolfrey at the other end of the table. A half-smile crossed Tom's face, then he nodded graciously, turned quickly and walked out. George followed.

2

*T*he new alliance of merchantmen presented a formidable problem. Strong though the Collective was, and gaining strength all
the time, the FC had neither the men nor the material to coordinate
a challenge to all merchantmen up and down the coast. Tom decided
to focus the Collective's energies on only one of the fishing houses;
Woolfrey's, partly because Woolfrey was the leader of the new
alliance, partly because Woolfrey had been the messenger, and partly
because Tom knew he would personally be in position on Our Island
to oversee all the actions against Woolfrey Enterprises.

The first action he planned, a march by men, women and
children on Woolfrey House, came to naught when it was learned
that Wes had sailed for his St. John's offices. By rights, Tom said, in
an offhand way, the FC should follow him to St. John's and confront
him there, but even as he said it he showed no real enthusiasm for
such a difficult project. Gradually, however, he warmed to the idea
of a public display of the FC on a great mission, and in the end there
was no part of the march that did not bear his mark.

If those papers owned and controlled by the merchantmen had
simply printed the truth — that the FC was marching on the St.
John's office of a northern house, then the people who read about it
would likely have seen the protest as a local problem, and let it go at
that. What happened instead was that the papers chose to publish
only parts of the story, and facts got tangled up in rumour. People
heard that the Collective was on the march to St. John's, but took
that to mean against the government.

With the government chronically out of favour and fishermen
everywhere once again discouraged by the poor price of fish, hun-

dreds, perhaps thousands, more people than those on the member-
ship rolls of the FC also joined the Great March.

'The Great March On St. John's.' It conjures up visions of
columns of fishermen, an army, making their way overland in a strict
regimented fashion. Nothing could be further from the truth. Tom
simply set a time for the fishermen of the Collective to meet him at
the Woolfrey Premises in St. John's. Some fishermen did walk to St.
John's, it is true, but more sailed than walked, and a good number
also came by train. Many stayed with family or friends and so
disappeared into the general population, an invisible force of uncertain number.

Before ever setting foot in St. John's, though, the FC had sent
around petitions calling for wholesale changes in the management of
the fisheries. Then, when the FC was established in St. John's, in a
meeting that went unreported by the press, Tom placed before the
Minister of Fisheries a petition of over ten thousand names.

Wes and Madeline were in the dining room of the Woolfrey
residence on Circular Road, the house where, before he was married,
Wes had lived when in St. John's. In every respect the house was
modest compared to its neighbours and to Woolfrey House up
north. But, to Madeline, Woolfrey House was of such a grand scale
and formality that she often felt diminished and oppressed in it. She
preferred this smaller house. Here, as never in Woolfrey House, she
had the place to her liking — the picture she wanted on the
mantelpiece, the curtains, plants and flowers of her choice, and only
herself to please with the placement of doilies and the like. Whenever
she could, she chose to live here for as long as possible.

On this day, despite the warm aromas from Madeline's kitchen,
Wes's meal had gone cold on his plate, not only untouched but
hardly noticed. Elbow on the table, hand supporting his head, he
gazed steadily at nothing in particular, lost in thought.

Madeline ate her own meal quietly, respectful of his contempla-
tion.

Without looking at her he said, "I have a meeting with the
Justice Minister, with Claude Caines."

She remembered him from the wedding, a small man with a tight thin smile. After offering her his congratulations, he slipped away from the festivities.

She glanced at the black-and-white photograph standing on the mantelpiece. Her eyes, then her thoughts, lingered for a moment on the picture of the newlyweds taken early the next morning.

In the weeks prior to the wedding in St. John's, both Madeline and her husband-to-be had exhausted themselves. By day, they threw themselves wholeheartedly into the preparations for the wedding, every night there were dinners and parties to attend.

On a sunny Saturday afternoon in June, they were married.

Despite their fatigue, however, neither could sleep that night, not even after lovemaking. Before dawn on Sunday morning, they were still awake, lying in the Grand Hotel's giant wedding bed. She sensed his restlessness, while the darkness and her weariness fed her own ruminations. Though the wedding was over, she worried, illogically, that she had overlooked some vital detail of the prenuptial arrangements. Though her body craved rest, her mind raced on, checking, re-checking. So used had she become to thinking like this in the weeks leading up to the wedding, she could not now turn it off. When it became intolerable, she threw the cool silk sheets back, went to the window and parted the curtains.

Summer stars were bright. Through the window screen a breeze breathed on her skin.

When she went back to bed, she piled and bunched the pillows so she could lie comfortably and look out at the stars at the same time. Before long Wes moved close to her. Perhaps she dozed, for the darkness lightened in abrupt steps. Outside, birds began to whistle and peep.

"Wes?"

"Um?"

She sighed. "There's not a single thing we *must* do today."

He was silent a moment. She felt him nod his head.

They were both silent.

She turned to face him just as he lifted up on his elbow the better to see her. Face to face they both began to speak at the same moment, their words flooding out, turning and tangling, tripping and repeating, and at about the same moment they realized how incomprehensible to the other they were. They both began to laugh.

The bridal suite was full of light.

"One thing I was trying to suggest," Madeline said, "we should go for a walk."

"Now?"

Madeline nodded. "Yes!" She sprang out of bed and softly ran to the window. "It's a beautiful morning. And it's so early there's not a soul about. It's Sunday! There won't be anyone around for hours. We'll have the city to ourselves. I've been here for weeks and I feel I haven't seen anything but the hotel, the dressmaker's and the sweet shop. Please, Wes, take me for a walk. Please, *husband*. Please."

Wes considered for only an instant. "An excellent idea, *wife*."

The night before, before they'd taken leave of their guests, Madeline had changed out of her splendid wedding dress and re-entered the ballroom wearing a shining turquoise silk dress of ankle length. Wes wore the dark brown, immaculately tailored suit in which he'd taken his vows. Only a few minutes after leaving the Grand Hotel, they returned, by a devious roundabout route, to the bridal suite, where the dress Madeline had not long ago put on slid easily off her shoulders to the floor.

Wearing those same clothes — Wes sans collar and tie — they stepped out into the brilliant summer morning.

They strolled aimlessly, arm-in-arm, chatting and laughing easily. As Madeline had predicted, the streets were empty. Her laughter sounded out through the early morning quiet as if such mornings were made especially for such delicate laughter.

Ever so gently Wes guided Madeline to Circular Road, huge Victorian-style houses dominating one side, the green manicured lawns of Government House rolling away on the other. Far down the road, where it appeared to end in a thicket of small trees, they spied someone, doing what, they could not be sure. As they got closer, they saw it was a man and a child standing side by side, the man with his hand on the child's shoulder. Closer still, they saw it was not a child at all, but a camera, on which the man's hand was resting. On the side of the camera: "R.A. Pike, Photographer."

A man of small build with a bushy moustache, Pike wore a jacket frayed at the wrists, his trousers at the cuffs. He tipped his bowler hat.

"It's early to be at work," Wes said.

The photographer smiled, lifted eyes and hand to the sky at the same moment. "The light," he said. "The light. The light this morning is perfect for my work." He lowered his hand, studied the two of them. "I am taking a picture of the road to put on postcards — they are very popular." Having said so much, he said no more, but continued to look at them and smile, as if, having explained himself, it was their turn to do likewise.

"We are . . ." Madeline began, "we *were* married . . . last evening."

Pike's eyebrows rose high in delight. Pointing at them as if to give instruction, he said, without hesitation, "Then you must have your picture taken this morning! In honour of such a wonderful occasion. There will be no charge."

Madeline and Wes protested, but Pike would hear none of it. He checked the light over his shoulder, repositioned the camera. Told them where to stand. By the time they struck a pose, Pike had seen the moment between moments, had already opened the shutter and captured it.

Weeks later, the picture arrived in the mail.

Wes stands with his jacket open and held back by the hand jammed in his trousers' pocket. His shirt is open-necked, his suit rumpled enough to take the formality out of it. His smile is wide and genuine. He is looking into Madeline's eyes and she into his. Her smile is open and natural. His left arm is over her shoulders, pulling her close. Her hand rests lightly on his jacket, over his heart.

A few minutes later, perhaps less than a hundred feet from where the picture was taken, Wes led Madeline up a set of wooden steps to this very house.

"I remember the Justice Minister."

Wes nodded.

"You will give him my regards?"

Without moving his head, Wes looked at her from the corners of his eyes. He said, "Now that he knows I'm going to meet with him, I'm sure the Minister just can't wait to know whether or not *you* are sending your regards."

She sat back straight in her chair. "I'm sorry," she said after a moment. "I don't understand. Have I said something wrong?"

"You think Claude Caines gives a damn? About you? Or me, for that matter?"

"Courtesy, Wes. I only mean to be courteous."

"That will solve everything."

"Something's wrong. I don't understand."

"No. You're right. You don't," he said. He stood up from the table. "With all that's going on here, all these people marching into town" — gradually he was speaking louder, more histrionically — "all these people, God only knows how many, marching down, following me from the north threatening who knows what, capable of causing trouble of God only knows what kind ... and *you* ... have to ask *me* ... what's *wrong*?" He shook his head, her failure to understand beyond his belief.

She stood, about to leave the room. Wes whipped his arm out, pointed at her, pinning her with his eyes where she stood.

"Explain them to me," he demanded. "For years they have lived off the Woolfreys and no one else. For years. And now, this. This ... this ... *march!*"

She raised her eyebrows, frightened. He let his arm fall to his side.

"*Explain it to me!*" he suddenly shouted, fists clenched, spittle flying. He said, as he advanced on her, grinning wickedly, "You know them, lived with them."

"Wes — "

"Why are they doing this? Tell me. You should know." Now they were face-to-face.

"Wes," Madeline said evenly, "I am your wife."

Her words surprised, then puzzled him. The grin disappeared. His features softened. He wanted to say something, but found no words. Then he did not know where to look.

Shamefaced, silently, he turned away, left the room.

Anthony, Claude Caines' secretary, met Wes on the steps of the Colonial Building, and led him away back down the steps and on around to the rear of the building, to a back door. Anthony was tall and thin and had to bend to unlock the door, which he held open for Wes. It was a spacious office. Standing in the doorway, Anthony nodded to a second, interior door, and told Wes to expect the Minister shortly, then he left.

The Minister does not want to be seen with me, Wes thought, looking around.

In every respect the office was well-appointed. A massive desk of cherry wood, brass lamps, deep comfortable chairs. Wes's eye was caught by a set of weather instruments hung on the wall opposite where he had entered. Half-a-dozen instruments in all, of which, on closer inspection, he was able to identify the dual scale thermometer, the barometer, and the hygrometer. On an instrument the likes of which he had never seen before, two small needles were tracing out a red line and a blue line on paper that very slowly, almost impercep-tibly, unrolled from one drum to another. Wes had no idea what it recorded, or why. He was admiring the instruments' gold casings when he heard a door open, then close. He turned around. Claude Caines, looking neither left nor right, hurried to the chair behind the desk and sat down. He was shorter and of a slighter build than Wes, and though the chair in which he sat was in appropriate proportion to the desk, it seemed greatly oversize with Caines sitting in it. Caines' eyes were small and hard behind wire-rimmed glasses, and they were looking straight into Wes's eyes. With a child-size hand, Caines motioned curtly to a chair in front of the desk, then leaned forward, elbows on the desk, hands laced in front of him, and watched as Wes crossed the room and sat. Caines was trembling as if in an effort to control some inner agitation. His face was thin and pointed, his mouth small, chin receding.

Wes made to speak, but Caines lifted a hand, brusquely shook his head.

Wes settled uneasily back in his chair, folded his hands in his lap. Caines bowed his head, laced his hands together, and looked for all the world as if he were about to say a prayer. Then he looked up and began to speak. His voice was surprisingly deep and smooth.

"All of a sudden, out of nowhere it seems, there is a 'Great March' and rumours of blockade — we are hearing all kinds of wicked rumours. Perhaps you should have given them a few pennies more for their cod.

"We do not know each other very well, Wes Woolfrey, but we have always been respectful of one another. What you think of me, or I of you, is of no great import, as long as we are equal in our respect for one another. You are of a class of men that I much admire. For many reasons. For your tenacity, for your willingness to take a risk, for knowing what you want out of life — I number many men just like you amongst my best and deepest friends. They are known to you, also. The brokers and bankers and businessmen of St. John's. They have their work and their lives here in the city, and you have yours in the north, and here in the city from time to time the two principalities meet, usually to mutual benefit. My friends have spoken highly of you and your family, of your business acumen, but, nowadays, Wes, they shake their heads. They wonder why you are bringing this trouble down on them from the north. They are angry, and they want me to tell you this dispute must be resolved as soon as possible. They believe we should all endeavour to deal with our problems at home. A new union is causing you trouble — so be it. We all have thorns in our sides, pebbles in our shoes. This union, this fellow Tom Vincent, caused no trouble down here until you brought him. I will remember his name. I do not forget the names of those who cause me trouble. You might do well to remember that yourself. For now, I leave him to you. He is your problem to solve.

"But if you cannot deal with him and his bloody union, then I will have to, and if this should be necessary, St. John's might become a more difficult business environment for you. If I have to solve this problem, everyone will pay. Not only the northern houses. Everybody. And they will blame you if they have to pay out higher prices. Nobody wants this, but it is known that I will not allow any solution to this problem to cost my government in any way.

"Out of nowhere, all of a sudden, fishermen from the north marching on government! My people, my government, will not take the brunt of this. I trust this is clear?"

Wes nodded. "Yes," he said hoarsely. He coughed to clear his throat. "Yes."

Caines nodded back. "Now," he said, "I have much to attend to. Please excuse me." He was already on his feet. As he headed for the door, he said, "Anthony will show you out." After a few more hurried steps he stopped, and quickly turned to Wes, who was still sitting.

Caines smiled. "Kindest regards to Madeline," he said.

The FC placed fishermen carrying signs of protest at the end of every pier in St. John's harbour. When they were ordered off private properties, they obeyed, but stood in boats alongside the piers and none could send them away.

But all to no great effect, it seemed.

So Tom called a public meeting.

3

From *The Evening Mail*

'GREAT MARCH' ENDS
IN UNION TRIUMPH

Government Sets Universal Price
For Fish To End Union Protest

ST. JOHN'S — Acting Justice Minister Claude Caines announced early this morning that legislation to set a Universal Minimum Price for Fish was approved last night during an emergency meeting of the Legislative Council. 'It is the fervent desire of this Government,' a tired Caines said, 'to put an end to the protests and riotous behaviour of the past week, so we have legislated a minimum price that must be paid for fish.' The exact value of the Universal Minimum Price will be revealed tomorrow when full details of the legislation are expected to be made public. It is understood, however, that the Universal Minimum Price is acceptable to all involved. Not as high as the Fishermen's Collective demanded, it is substantially more than brokers and merchants were originally willing to pay. Expect the full particulars in tomorrow's edition of *The Evening Mail.*

The emergency meeting was called last evening after a week of bitter protests climaxed yesterday afternoon when hundreds of angry fishermen brandishing clubs and firing shotguns into the air roamed up and down Water Street causing all businesses there to cease operation for the remainder of the day. The week-long blockade of the harbour by Union boats continued meanwhile to disrupt all regular shipping activity. The fishermen bring a long list of grievances against the government and the fish companies, the low price paid for fish (prior to last evening's agreement) being chief amongst them.

Brief skirmishes with the police resulted in only minor injuries to both sides, but the far outnumbered and unarmed policemen generally left the protesters free to do as they pleased. Fires were set in the street. No arrests were made.

Earlier in the day, speaking to a crowd of about fifteen hundred, Tom Vincent, President of the Fishermen's Collective, had criticized the government for being tardy in dealing with issues of life and death consequence to fishermen. He also declared that he was 'disappointed and disheartened' by what he had seen of a proposal being prepared by government, with the backing of the fish merchants, to end the fishing strike. Vincent told the crowd the proposal was 'scrabbled together — lacking in both insight and foresight,' and it was after this speech that the fishermen moved downtown. It was only after he spoke to the crowd again, many hours later, that the riot ended. In his second speech, delivered well after dark from the balcony of Hardy's Saddlery, where he was illuminated by torchlight, Vincent told the Unionists it was time to go home. He strengthened the resolve of the expectant crowd to do just that by telling them that the Legislative Council was in session even as he spoke and that he would soon have 'good news for all.' He suggested that their mission was near accomplished and that the strike could be over 'within a day or two — hours, perhaps, if we have good fortune.' The crowd roared its approval, and as soon as Vincent was gone from the balcony, the street began to empty of the weary but jubilant protesters. Thus the riot came to an end last night, and the 'good news' for fishermen came, as promised, just a few hours later.

Politicians on both sides of Government, the general public, and St. John's fishermen (few of whom have been members of the Fishermen's Collective until now), had been speaking out all week against the Collective's bullying and strong-arm tactics which obviously culminated in yesterday's riot. Earlier this week Non-Unionists told of being dragged off main streets into alleys where they were punched and kicked and called names and then sent away bruised, and ofttimes bloodied, with warnings to support the FC or to suffer the consequences. Three Non-Union boats were mysteriously holed and sunk mid-week and there were numerous complaints from the St. John's men of damaged gear. The number of these incidents decreased dramatically once the St. John's fishermen met with Union leaders and decided either to join up or cease opposing the striking fishermen. 'The ruffians and vandals responsible for these attacks,' Tom Vincent said after the meeting, 'are cowardly by nature and will now think twice before acting against individuals to whom the Fishermen's Collective has promised protection.'

Plans have been announced for a Grand Victory Celebration to be held on the grounds of the Colonial Building tomorrow afternoon. 'Our protest is over, our battle won,' Tom Vincent said. 'Now we are all for celebration, but we want this Government to feel the press of our people at their doors. We want them to know that, if the details of this agreement do not meet our needs, then we will be back, stronger and more defiant.'

4

Celebration the furthest thing from his mind that day. No room in his head for that, for anything but headache.

Kept his eyes closed.

Begun in the right temple — when was that? — speaking to the crowd? First time he spoke to them yesterday, losing them. No. They were restless, but he wasn't losing them, no. Not losing them. Understood they were in a foul mood, surly. Making their way, must have been cold, uncomfortable, for more than a week, and what they had done to men and boats, done, had to be, but still nothing to show. Primed they were to end it all, for sure, one way or another. A matter of time only, before all would out and God Help You then if you stood in their way. Standing before them, directed at him or not, he knew that, felt it too. Afraid of losing them, and at that very moment, pain in the right temple.

Then George, broad-shouldering and bullying, ploughing his way into the crowd, elbows swinging, knocking his way through, and with the flat of his hand slapping some fellows hard, hard, hard on the back, punching others on the arm, and glaring at them all fearlessly and insulting them for not doing enough and challenging them to do more. Roused them up generally every way he knew how, and when they came back at him, cursing him, or with their own fists raised and ready to pound, George shouted, "Not me, Friend! Not me! Down there," he flung an arm, "on Water Street, there's your foe!" Then he pointed to the platform, to Tom, "Listen to the man, my friend, listen!"

Tom did not think at all about what he said, but — did they work together like that, hand and glove? — George on a loose ramble through the crowd, as the pain slow-seeped into his head like a shadow, and Tom was as frightened then of what might happen as he was fiercely troubled now thinking about what might have.

His guts tore at him.

The vinegar plant did nothing this day to ease the pain.

But the whisky, once he started to keep it down, worked wonders.

5

The crowd started to gather early in front of the Colonial Building. The Legislature, judiciously, perhaps, had cancelled its session on this day of celebration.

Fishermen carried signs and placards. Townspeople were there, and soldiers and sailors, and policemen in uniform, all caught up in the excitement, smiling and backslapping and chattering.

Cans o' the 'shine ghosted through the crowd.

Tom arrived — the people's darling then. They sent up a great roar of welcome and pressed towards him.

They all wanted to see him and touch him and cheer him on. Tom did all that was expected of him and more. He moved slowly towards the steps of the Colonial Building. He shook people's hands, smiled, nodded and waved to them. He allowed himself to be buffeted about and gently roughed up. When he was through, he took the steps two at a time, smiling and waving still, and the crowd's roaring went on and on and on.

He gave them an inspired victory speech. The crowd was joyous and interrupted frequently to cheer and applaud. That was the kind of afternoon it was.

Tom and George stood on the uppermost steps of the building, between two of the great columns supporting the portico. Tom paused to drink water from a bottle that George had brought for that purpose, then turned and looked at the doors of the building. Closed tight. His look travelled up the great dull blank wall. He lifted the bottle to his lips. Facing the door and the wall he took a long drink. He wiped his mouth on the sleeve of his jacket. He tilted his head to one side, then to the other, quick movements, up and down in the manner of a small puzzled animal and finally he looked at George, handing the bottle back to him.

Tom's face was bright with a delighted knowingness. He nodded his head towards the Legislature doors. "The day will come, Mr. Gill, when we will rouse the beast within!"

The roll call in their meetings, the Change Islands Council wrote, always began with the President's name. *Tom Vincent?* To which any member present would respond *Here!* They wanted to know if this was an acceptable protocol.

Tom shrugged. "Fine," he said.

It soon became the standard practice of most councils.

7

Madeline's long heavy coat did not keep out the chilling wind. The cold mist that blew steadily against her face was numbing, but she chose to stand on the open bow of the *WW* heading for the Outer Islands. The chill in the wind and the mist was both emotional anaesthetic and mental stimulant. The combination gave her thinking an edge she needed.

One of the older menservants from Woolfrey House was at the wheel. Swinging a window out and holding it up with one hand, holding the wheel with the other, he stretched out into the weather and called to her again. "Mrs. Woolfrey!" When she turned, hair dangling in wet curls about her face, her face dripping wet and white from the cold, her eyes in contrast were brightly brown and beautiful.

He motioned her inside.

She shook her head. After a moment, raising her voice a little, she said, "Thank you for taking me out, Gray."

He bowed his head, knowing he'd done only as Wes had ordered. She needn't have said anything, though, so he appreciated the thanks. He was glad to be out of the house anyway, and on the water for a good change.

"My pleasure, Ma'am, but I'd feel better if you joined me inside."

"I'm fine," she said, trying to smile, then turned and stood as she had been, pulled her collar a little tighter around her neck. Gray withdrew from the window, and latched it with a sympathetic shiver.

It was only a matter of time, Madeline knew.

Was it the severity of the weather that worked against her being able to bring to mind, even fleetingly, anything pleasant from her marriage?

It was the cold, she knew for sure, that framed startling clear images of eye and tooth that were the very concentrate of her pain.

As long as she stayed with Wes, she would be in peril.

They'd hardly spoken for a week.

She'd tried to learn to live with his casual philandering, though of late she almost wished she didn't know. But he had made no attempt to spare her that knowledge and that pain. Her upset, he assured her, served only to demonstrate her *naivete*.

Early on, she'd spent long hours studying accounting the better to understand the nature of her husband's work, so as to be a help to him. At first Wes was delighted by the romantic notion of it, but soon he had no choice but to praise her quick mind. He came to trust her with important accounts. Now, her expertise with numbers was all he ever asked of her. He was as indifferent to her, otherwise, as to any of the hired help.

When she pleaded with him, he chuckled.

She told him how she longed to be with him. She cast her mind back to the Outer Islands and presented the idea to him as calmly, as genuinely, and as laden with sexual promise as she could.

He'd pointed outside, to the miserable cold and misty afternoon, asked her how any right thinking person could make such a suggestion on such a day?

No need to get out of the boat at all, she answered, still hopeful.

Then go by yourself, he said.

I will, she hissed, hurt, but defiant.

She was close to him by then, face-to-face, and suddenly, with no warning sign at all, he raised his fist and snarled at her. His curling lip exposed the canine. There was blood rage in his eye. The images kept returning to her now. She couldn't get them out of her mind.

She knew he would strike her one day.

It was only a matter of time before he hurt her. He'd restrained himself this time, he'd lowered his hand, but he was still angry when he turned and swung the door open, called for Gray and gave him the orders.

Gray was now pulling the tender up on the beach. Madeline stepped out into the soft and soggy sand, the mist thick and cold about her. She took one look around. There was nowhere to go, so she climbed back into the tender.

"Take me home," she said.

Back on the *WW* she stood in the wheelhouse, shivering. The cold had gone so deep that even after she went below, changed her wet clothes and wrapped herself in blankets, even then there was neither warmth nor comfort.

PART V

*I*n the November election of 1913, for the first time ever, the Fishermen's Collective ran campaigns in the thirteen constituencies known as 'The Northern Districts.' Tom Vincent, President of the FC, ran in the District of Our Island.

Then, as now, the story of elections in Newfoundland was almost always of what happened in the St. John's districts, St. John's being the capital of the country, its most populous city, and the centre of trade. That the Fishermen's Collective was fielding candidates in the Northern Districts was considered by the editors of *The Evening Mail* to be an unusual but insignificant development. After all, the incumbents in those districts were on the Government side of the House at dissolution, some even in Cabinet, and Tom Vincent and his FC had not been much in the news since their 'Great March.' Still, any new political development made the editors uneasy. To assuage their mild anxieties, they sent their most inexperienced reporter north.

It was the worst possible assignment for Hammond Janes. He was in his late twenties and had just laid down his coopering tools in hopes of bettering himself as a newspaperman. Though full of energy and optimism, he had much to learn, and was looking forward to learning on-the-job, working with more experienced hands. Instead, he was sent north on his own, his only instruction being not to phone or wire copy, but to use the first available mail.

In those Northern Districts the mail was as uncertain as the St. John'smen were sure the outgoing government would be returned to power.

. . .

Hammond set out to meet as many candidates in as many districts as possible, but in district after district the sitting Members of the House of Assembly felt so confident of re-election that they campaigned hardly at all. Some made token visits to their districts, others did not. As little in evidence as government members were, opposition candidates were even less so. Unofficially they'd already conceded victory to the incumbents and were not willing even to show for the fight.

Not knowing what else to do, Hammond travelled on, meeting the people.

Before this trip he'd spent little time in fishing villages. Being from St. John's, a "townie" through and through, and the son of a cooper, he knew little of the daily round of the fisherman's life. His father's work often took him to out-harbours near St. John's, and there was a time when Hammond was a child that he clamoured like crazy to travel there with his father. After a few visits, however, he tired of the tiny ramshackle settlements and the generally dour demeanour of the people, and as he grew older he visited these places less often. To Hammond's eyes, they remained colourless and unchanging, as poor and as needy as ever.

Now, in the Northern Districts, Hammond boarded wherever he could find a place. There were few amenities, but the houses he stayed in were warm and clean and the people prided themselves on feeding him well. No one goes hungry around here anymore, they told him, not since Tom Vincent got the good prices for fish, not since the Great March.

These people might not be fully satisfied with their lives, but Hammond observed that they were content, at least, and busy. Everyone who wanted to work, worked. Still, they struck Hammond as a glum lot until he learned that last winter's bout of consumption had taken many lives. Then he understood that they were in the latter days of their grief, the election of a new government far from their minds.

But when he did ask them about it, they told him they knew the members looking for re-election would, as always, be paying little attention to them, and it followed that if the politicians ignored them during the election, what could be expected of them once they made up the government? Didn't Claude Caines, the Acting Justice Minister who had become Prime Minister, didn't he have a solid majority in government with over a year to go before he had to call an election? For whatever reason he'd decided to call the election now, you could be sure it had nothing to do with the people. Early on, almost everybody Hammond met expected the government to go back in just the same — what with the corruptions and scandals and the disrespect the politicians of all parties had for the electorate, there was no reason to choose one party or politician over another. The devil you know is better than the one you don't.

Hammond first sensed the birthing vibration of something new in the voice of an old salt who told him he was waiting for a visit from Tom Vincent and the FC candidate.

And what do you expect of him? Hammond had asked.

"We'll see," the fisherman answered. "But in the years he have run the FC, he have worked wonders for the fishermen on this coast and no one's likely to forget that."

Then, in a village that Tom Vincent, George Gill and an FC candidate had visited just the evening before, the fishermen told Hammond straight out: "We're votin' FC."

Hammond climbed back in the boat and caught up with Tom in Leading Line.

When Tom Vincent of the Fishermen's Collective was speaking, the meeting halls were always crowded. FC flags, blue with the stylized white cod in the centre, hung from every wall. Most men wore buttons bearing the same emblem and many wore dark-blue guernseys. By then there was such a close association between the guernsey and the FC that, simply wearing it anywhere working conditions were difficult, had come to be seen as an act of defiance.

Hammond was surprised by the number of women. They had no vote, after all, yet showed up in numbers such as turned out to church services.

When Tom Vincent, George Gill, and the FC candidate entered suddenly through a side door, everybody stood and the applause was solid, long and loud.

Hammond stood near the back of the hall that first evening and craned his neck to see them. There was no doubting which of the three on the platform was Tom Vincent: broad-shouldered with black hair falling in loose curls. Although his cheeks were pock-marked and pitted, he looked younger than Hammond expected. He had a broad bright smile.

Sometimes he wore a suit, and at other times, as on the first evening Hammond saw him, he wore the guernsey. He always displayed an FC button over his heart. He took to the stage confidently and was comfortable there, smiling and nodding to the crowd. He let the gathering take a good long look before assuming his seat and it was only then that the roar of welcome subsided.

After the three were formally introduced to the crowd, the candidate made a brief speech, a cross between declaration of candidacy and a record of involvements and works with the FC. The candidate's last duty was to introduce Tom and, as he sat, to accept part of Tom's applause as his own.

Tom stood.

When it was silent, and he began to speak, some golden presence entered the room in and through his voice.

"Not long ago," he began, his voice carrying out strong and clear into the expectant air, "I was talking to my good friend Noah Torraville, just up the coast here. He is known to many of you and those of you that do not know him have probably heard of him. A good man, Noah. A hard worker. A God-fearing man who is not afraid to speak his mind or to tell it as he sees it. If you do not know him or have not heard of him, then for sure you know someone like him for tonight there are many like him, here, in this hall.

"My friends, Noah was telling me he remembers the time when he was First Mate on a schooner in a fleet of twelve preparing for the Labrador. When the Chief Purser for the fleet tallied up who had bought what in preparation for the voyage, one cape ann was found missing, taken that is, but not paid for, and no one would own up to it, no one would come forward and confess to the error. What happened then, Noah said, was near unbelievable, but Noah assures me this is a true story. Because the one offender was unknown, every man that sailed in that fleet of ships that season had his wages docked by the price of one new cape ann.

"Who, my friends, is the more shamed by this: is it the merchantman who charges all to pay for the single misdeed? Or is it the schoonermen who paid without a word of protest?" Tom paused, holding up his hand to forestall an answer. "No matter, my friends, no matter. Not any more. The point of Noah's story when he told it to me was that no merchant would attempt any such a thing on this coast again because of our Fishermen's Collective — and isn't that the truth?" The crowd confirmed him with a solid round of applause. "Noah, I said a little later in our conversation, you've been a member of the FC for a long time? Oh yes, Mr. President (Noah is very respectful), oh yes, Mr. President, he answered . . . but not right from the start. What do you mean? I asked. Well, he said, the first time I heard you talk about the FC, I knew it would never work, I knew it could never last, and I was sure and certain it would never accomplish anything . . . but I joined up after the Great March. I have to admit I was wrong about the FC. So, Noah, I said, you thought our march was a good idea. Oh no! Noah replied, not at the time. That was a terrible idea! Any fool could see that wouldn't work! You didn't have to be an educated man to see that a march wouldn't accomplish anything . . . but I guess I have to admit I was wrong about the march, too. Well, Noah, I said, I'm down here today to tell the people that the FC is going to run men in this election. Now, what do you think of that? Noah thought about it, oh, for maybe a minute. Well, Mr. President, he finally said, with all due respect, that must be the silliest idea of all." Tom let it hang a moment. "And I said to Noah: Thank you very much, Noah, I was worried to death you might say it could work!"

All of a sudden it was a room full of laughter.

He was one of them, no doubt. He spoke their language, perfectly. What he said, he said for them, as they themselves would have said it, if they'd the mind for talk — only a few have that gift, but they all knew the rightness and truth of what was in their hearts and Tom knew what was in their hearts too. You could tell, because he had the mind for words. When he spoke, he spoke of right and true things.

In places like this, full of flags and buttons and guernseys, Tom Vincent had become the outward sign of the inward people.

Tom went on to talk about the progress of the FC. He praised the people for the mighty works they had accomplished, then he spoke plainly the litany of simple things that were yet to do:

"We need to standardize our grading of fish and we need government-trained Fish Inspectors and we need, have fought and are still fighting for, a higher universal fixed price for our fish. And we all know our communities need schools and there should be at least one telephone in every community, and our people need old age pensions and a minimum wage and hospitals, not just a doctor here and there. Hospitals, my friends. Did not last winter's cruelty prove this out once again? And it goes without saying the current corrupt practices of government need investigation — but these are not the main issues in this election. The politicians in St. John's do not talk fish cull or minimum wage. Your own members — and you know this is true, for sure — they do not speak to your issues, if they speak at all. No. In this election there is only one issue. And it is this: whether or not *we* — *you and I* — are going to take this election seriously."

He gave them a moment to think.

"Oh things can go as they've gone before. We can send the members back and forget about them . . . and, sadly, until the next election, they'll forget about us. Or, as we did at the founding of the Fishermen's Collective, not so many years ago, we can once again become the thin edge of the wedge of reform. We can make our issues government issues — but it starts here with you." Pointing. "You must vote, and you must vote . . . and you must vote, for your FC candidate."

Tom swept his arm in the candidate's direction and the candidate, who had waited anxiously for this cue, sprang to his feet. Tom applauded him and the crowd followed Tom's lead. He easily coaxed them to their feet, gestured to them to stamp, to whistle and cheer, and then, after a humble nod to acknowledge the crowd's enthusiasm for his own work, he stepped back and turned to further deflect the crowd's good will towards the smiling, shuffling FC candidate.

The spell of the speech, not only what was said but also the rhythm of it, captivated Hammond Janes as easily as it did everyone else. When Tom finished, Hammond clapped and cheered without thinking, then realized with a start how easily he'd been entranced. The next moment he went silent, shoved his hands deep into his trouser pockets.

By the time Hammond pushed through to the front of the hall, Tom was nowhere to be seen. But he saw George Gill standing guard near a door.

Somewhat cowed by George's blockiness, the size of his hands, Hammond approached and said, "I would like to speak to Mr. Vincent."

"And who might you be?" George asked.

"A reporter with *The Evening Mail*," Hammond said.

George nodded. "Very good," he said. "You can see him after those two." George gestured in the direction of a short gray-haired woman wearing a dark coat, the hem nearly touching the floor. Her left hand was wrapped in a thick white bandage, darkly blotched. Behind her stood a younger woman with a baby on her shoulder. The baby's breath was thick, wet and laboured. The mother kept patting its back. Hammond took his place in line.

The door opened but Hammond could not see in. A fisherman came out, chuckling. George let the old woman in. She came out a minute later, bandage gone, and Tom calling after her to "leave it open to the air, my dear, that's all."

Mother and child were admitted, and were inside for some time. Hammond could hear the baby crying, then coughing, and as the hall emptied and became quieter, a soft rhythmic slapping could sometimes be heard coming from inside the room. The baby was asleep on the woman's shoulder when they came out.

George followed Hammond in, shut the door behind him.

"That's all," George said. "This man's a reporter from St. John's."

Tom was half-sitting, half-leaning, on the edge of a table.

"Do you know anything?" Tom asked.

The question was unexpected, and Hammond was just as surprised to hear Tom speak to him in the accent of a St. John'sman, much different than the one he'd just been using.

After a long moment Hammond answered, "Yes. I suppose so — I mean," he added quickly, "this is my first assignment as a reporter, on my own I mean, but I know some things."

"Well, that puts you ahead of the rest," Tom said. "I've been written up many times before. In the FC newspaper I've been done full and fair, but as for the others — some good, mostly bad. But you're the first one of their reporters who wanted to speak to me." He gave Hammond a devilish grin. "Who owns you?"

"*The Mail*," Hammond said. "I mean — they don't own me, sir. I work for them."

"Yes. Well. We'll see, won't we? What's your name, son?"

"Hammond — "

"Hammond! We'll see, won't we, Hammond? We've been doing great work down here, lately, Hammond, but no one in the capital has noticed, or cares very much about it. That's to our advantage though. We'd just as soon catch them unawares. The FC is going to put members in the House of Assembly this election and that's not bombast. And you'll have the privilege of being a witness to that — and note I said *members* — more than one. My advice to you, son, is that you try to write some of what I'm saying down so you don't forget it."

Hammond fumbled through his pockets for a pencil.

Tom spoke to him then for five, ten, fifteen minutes. About the Fishermen's Collective. The election. Hammond scribbled furiously to keep up but still missed much of what was said. Head down, Tom paced slowly back and forth in front of the table, then circled Hammond once, twice, looking at him now and then to emphasize a point.

When George opened the door, Tom nodded to Hammond and walked out, left him there, still scribbling, not a single question asked.

For the rest of the campaign Hammond tracked Tom and his candidates. From time to time Tom would turn to him and talk politics, but it was only after he had his say that he'd answer Hammond's questions. In this manner they spoke in smoky halls, in cold open boats, in warm and friendly kitchens full of fishermen.

Tom supplied Hammond with back issues of *The Fishermen's Rejoinder*. In them, there was far more information on Tom and the rise of the FC than Hammond needed, and it was oft-repeated. But Hammond read and studied those papers anyway, until he practically knew the FC's version of their own history by heart.

And slowly, carefully, Hammond wrote and re-wrote his stories until he felt they presented a very reasonable, unbiased, and objective picture of Tom's campaign through the Northern Districts.

One story after another he wrote. Regular as clockwork, he sent them off.

"They don't publish your stories, son," Tom said to Hammond one afternoon before hurrying to another packed and expectant hall.

"I don't know," Hammond replied. "I don't have copies yet to check."

Without missing a step or taking his eyes off Hammond, Tom made a motion with his hand. George gave him a sheaf of folded newspapers.

Tom stopped. Everyone stopped.

In a smooth motion, in a friendly, familiar manner, he pushed the newspapers against Hammond's chest. He said, "These are the most recent issues. We're not in them, or any of the earlier issues. I don't know what they're paying you for, son. They never print what you write."

Then Tom turned on his heel and strode off to meet the people.

Hammond stood and watched him go.

From then on Hammond was not one of those to whom Tom

turned to speak. And as Tom did, so did his entourage. Hammond travelled with them still, but as one apart.

As election day approached, Hammond wrote and wrote with a certain desperation. He wanted something he wrote — anything — to be published. He needed this now, he realized, to prove something to himself, and to prove something to Tom — especially to Tom. But still none of his work appeared.

He wrote letters asking why, and no one answered. He sent a wire. Silence.

In the last report he wrote before election day, he predicted an FC sweep of the thirteen districts, eight of which he'd visited with Tom.

After he looked at what he'd written, he laughed out loud. It was his first election, after all, and during the campaign he'd only ever seen Tom and the FC candidates. He really knew little more than the names of those the FC were running against and he'd had no help at all, no mentor to discuss things with. In the end, Hammond trusted to intuition and made his prediction. He was confident that, like the rest of his work, it would go unpublished.

When the election results were known, the FC victories were declared spectacular and unprecedented. All thirteen FC candidates, just as Hammond had predicted, had been elected.

On the first Sunday after voting day, in a Special Election Supplement, all of Hammond's stories, hitherto relegated to a high and mainly unread stack on a junior editor's desk, appeared as "The Chronicle of the Fishermen's Collective Campaign."

The supplement had to be reprinted.

Tom bought and sent copies to every council of the Collective.

2

When Tom returned to St. John's as newly elected Member of the House of Assembly, he spent the first night in a rented room on New Gower Street. The next morning he tended to the graves of his mother and father, and that afternoon he explored the Colonial Building.

He sat for a long while in the Strangers' Gallery of the Legislative Assembly. The windows were high and the room full of light which caught on cornice and column and the elaborate ornamentation of Empire. It rested on the arms and legs and high backs of all the polished chairs and tables, government and opposition, still facing each other in near-equal numbers as at dissolution.

Now thirteen of those chairs would go to the FC.

He had a quick look at the office he'd been assigned. It was simply too small. He wanted a place that would be both constituency *and* FC office, and part living quarters, too, if he could get it.

That evening he bought a newspaper. Eight pages, with advertisements, none offering office space. To find the kind of place he needed, he'd have to visit businesses and buildings individually. He decided to start first thing next morning at the east end of Water Street, the end closest to the Colonial Building.

When he stepped out of the hotel early that morning, the November sun was bright and the morning air unseasonably warm and close. Down in the harbour, schooner spars stood tall and dark against the sun-flash on the water, and the early morning sounds carried a long way in the quiet.

He started down to Water Street feeling in himself the excitement of a new beginning. When he did not keep it down, the thought that intoxicated him was that he and the other twelve FC members would hold the balance of power in the new government.

He first made inquiries at a two-story building. The ground floor sold 'General Provisions' but the second story, showing blank and uncurtained windows, looked to be unoccupied.

The owner of the building and proprietor of the store were one and the same: a big round-faced man with mutton-chop sideburns. He sat alert and contented behind his cash register and listened carefully as Tom explained what he was looking for.

And yes, the space above was available.

Tom's good mood heightened with the possibility of finding what he needed first place he asked.

The proprietor waddled out from behind the register. He locked the door with a big key, then hung a 'Closed' sign in the window. He held out a plump hand and said, "Now I'd be glad to show you the upstairs, Mister . . ."

"Tom Vincent," Tom said, shaking the hand.

"Oh!" the businessman said. "Oh! Not from that damn Collective?" And he glared at Tom as if he thought it physically impossible for Tom Vincent to be made flesh in his own store.

"The same," Tom said.

The proprietor snatched the sign out of the window, clumsily unlocked the door because he could not steady the key in his hand. Then he swung the door open and brusquely motioned for Tom to leave.

"Good day to you, sir," Tom said. He stepped out of the store into morning air even warmer and closer than before.

Tom loosened his tie. He took off his jacket, rolled up his shirt sleeves, then crossed the dry dusty street to ask about space at a saddlery, but there was nothing there.

He traipsed the length of Water Street that morning but he knew, not long after starting out, that no one would rent to him. Word that he was on the way, and what he was looking for, travelled down both sides of the street faster than he could walk.

In windows above tobacco and confectionery shops, people leaned out and stared down. In some doorways, men in blood-spattered aprons or sharp suits stood with arms crossed and tracked his slow progress.

He knew these people would not rent to him now, but he refused to give it up. The more he was turned away, the more determined he became to finish what he'd started.

He was a union man looking for a place on a merchantman's street. By mid-morning, his good mood gone and his white shirt stuck to him with sweat, he'd spoken to many young men and women, the sons and daughters of the founders of the businesses, and he thought it sad that so many of them already had hearts set hard in the way of merchantmen.

He willed himself to commit thoughts, details and feelings to memory, knowing that someday, somewhere, he'd tell the story of the time he walked from one end of Water Street to the other looking for a place to call his own.

That morning such imaginings of the future made him smile and lifted his spirits a little. In better humour, he made a sudden face at two women holding back curtains to look out at him. They jumped back, hands to their mouths.

He felt as if he'd knocked on every door on Water Street.

The street was crowded and busy now, his throat was dust-dry, but he was determined that none would see him falter.

A man pushing a wheelbarrow across the street wore a blue and white FC button over his heart.

Tom croaked out, "Friend!"

Hearing the call the man set his wheelbarrow down, looked at Tom.

"My Christ!" he said in sudden recognition. "Tom Vincent?"

Tom nodded. Before he could say a word, the man straightened up, his face a mask of proud defiance, and slapped the button on his chest with the palm of his hand.

"I never takes 'im off, Mr. Vincent," he said solemnly, as if he'd been waiting to say that to someone for a long time. Then he stood there, not another word in his mouth.

"I need a drink," Tom said.

"I got 'shine."

"Water," Tom said. "I need water."

"That's easy," the man said. He hailed two of his mates and sent them off to fetch some water.

While they waited around a corner in a cool shed, Tom spoke of the trouble he was having finding a place to set up home and office.

The man stood silent, thinking. "I don't know if they'd be fitting for your purposes," he said, "but there is more buildings, about a mile along, a few. I know one fellow's got some kind of a shop out there, even though it's out of the way. You might find something there."

Cold and clear the water in the bucket. Tom ladled it out, drank his fill.

'R. A. Pike, Photographer' read the sign above a high brick building on a narrow tree-lined lane.

On both sides of the lane, behind the trees, there were empty abandoned houses, each wearing a necklace of broken glass and nondescript rubbish. Even the grounds around the building had been neglected, allowed to go wild, but the building itself stood solid and proud, the centrepiece of some failed ambition.

Pike the photographer, a small man with a bushy moustache and a shiny bald head, smelled of liquor. He wore a vest and arm bands and looked more like a gambler than a drinker.

Tom explained his need. If Pike recognized Tom's name, he gave no indication. He was a man of few words.

He guided Tom through the photographic paraphernalia littering the floor of the studio — frames and pans, tripods and reflectors, cameras and brown bottles of chemical stuff, to second and third floors as empty as the studio had been chaotic.

Light from high windows washed into rooms heavy with dust long trapped and dry.

Pike explained that he'd once planned to use the space to show his pictures . . . He shrugged.

Tom said he'd take both floors.

Pike nodded and suggested a drink to seal the deal. Tom declined. Pike shrugged again.

Tom had the two floors renovated just the way he wanted.

When it was finished, it looked as if he'd spared no expense.

The truth: he had paid his workers good wages, but when they discovered who'd hired them, they simply did better than their best work.

Tom now lived further from the Colonial Building than any other member of the House of Assembly. Before long he arranged for a car and driver to take him back and forth from the bottom of Pike's Lane to the Colonial Building on Military Road, and he let it be known that, for the cost of shared gas expenses, there was room for a small number of other passengers.

When he posted a schedule of his arrivals and departures on the door of his assigned but seldom used office at the Colonial Building, the word on the lips of the other politicians was, 'Undignified.'

More people than politicians, however, worked for government and among the secretaries and bookkeepers, cooks and cleaners, there were some who lived just as far from their work as Tom, some further. The car was fast and affordable, its one drawback being that it was not big enough.

Tom encouraged the driver to invest in a bigger vehicle. With the FC as a partner, he did just that, and after Tom brought in people from Union Cove and put them to work in his offices down Pike's Lane, the demand for the service and its success was assured.

The other passengers soon got used to sitting next to Tom the MHA, and for three years or so he squeezed between painters and carpenters and joked that he'd rather ride in cramped quarters with the whole honest lot of them than to sit across from a thieving politician. They roared at his self-mockery.

He brought people down from Our Island to run the FC offices and they needed places to live. With profits from the various FC enterprises, he bought the land and the houses down Pike's Lane. He had the shacks torn down and in their place raised the same simple style of house that had been built for his workers in Union Cove, and he rented the houses at Cove rates. No one would lose anything because he or she had to move to St. John's to live and work.

Someone opened a little store, then someone else another, and Pike's Lane was soon transformed. With everybody down the Lane working at one thing or another, it became a respectable and prosperous address.

Tom never forgot how useless the newspaper had been in his search for space to rent, so not long after he settled in at Pike's Lane, he brought out his own advertising sheet. It was very cheaply done, but the rental and all other information was as accurate as could be the morning it was published.

It meant some legwork on his part. Time, he soon discovered, that he needed for Government work.

But he wanted it done right, and in this enterprise as in so many others, he accepted that this meant doing it himself for a time. Once he got things going, once projects could run themselves, he'd hand the routine responsibility over to someone else.

So it was with the advertising sheet: within six months he gave it to a keen young man he'd hired in the first instance to gather information and distribute the sheet.

The sheet brought a profit to the Collective for years.

With his election to the House of Assembly in 1913, Tom moved from the wings of public recognition to centre stage. Had people recalled that for five years he had run Newfoundland's largest union, they would not have been as surprised by his sure and certain command of power.

True to his word, he brought the concerns of the fishermen to government. While the other parties puzzled out their roles and relative power in the new order of the House, Tom seized the moment and drove through legislation to increase the wages and improve the working conditions of loggers and sealers. His *Local Affairs Act* included a long-term plan for the construction of roads and schools and provided for immediate installation of phone service to all larger communities and extension of telegraph services to the smaller ones. He tried, but failed, to standardize the grading of fish. This reform, aimed as it was at changing the very nature of the fishery, was steadfastly opposed by both other parties, who in large part represented businessmen and fish brokers with vested interests in having things stay just as they were. So Tom had to settle, on this go-round, for the establishment of a minimum grade for exportable fish, and for the introduction of intensive government training for fish inspectors.

Detailed examinations of the previous government's records, now available to both the FC and the former opposition party, uncovered corruption almost everywhere. There were daily revelations of questionable dismissals, suspect hirings, misappropriation of funds, false expenditures — the offenses were numberless. Less so, but impressive nonetheless, were the number of former government members and officials forced out of office by the determined and coordinated campaign conducted in the House by the former opposition and the FC.

Prime Minister Caines, whose ostentatious and lavish lifestyle led many to believe that he was the most corrupt of all politicians, remained untouched and unscathed by the scandals. Between the Prime Minister and any allegation or suspicion of wrongdoing one always found the buffer of the Department of Justice, of which, everyone knew, the Prime Minister had been acting minister for years.

At first, Caines rose in the House on every appropriate occasion to offer spirited defenses of his colleagues. But as time wore on and the charges multiplied and the condemning evidence mounted, he sank into a sullen and abject silence, glaring steadily across the floor into the faces of the forces arrayed against him. The effect of his silence was to distance himself from the members of his own party and to communicate to them that it was every man for himself, his party suddenly in unforeseen and desperate disarray.

"I just got tired, you know.

"The moment we were the balance of power, all the decisions we had to make and all the votes we had to cast, they were all important, and we were all new to government, and although my men, every one of them, were good men, they were limited. I bore them no ill will for that. I knew who they were and what they were capable of when I ran them for election. So it was for me to decide on all issues, be they great or small.

"So the full weight of work in government did not so much fall *to* me as it fell *on* me. And to make a long story short, one night I knew I had to get out from underneath the weight of the world or I would perish there, so I jumped to my feet and followed George and the rest of them to Kerrywinkle's Social Club. That was our place to drink after the prohibition was forced on us in 1915. There! That's what I mean: in 1913 we were the balance of power. When the war broke out, we had to negotiate the Coalition, and then came the prohibition referendum, and having a part in all that — in what? —

twenty-four months — would wear out any man, take it from me, for sure and for certain.

"Anyway no one was more surprised than George when I walked into Kerrywinkle's that first time.

"That place was forever loud and crowded and thick with smoke and the piano always out of tune and always under some kind of assault.

"The ceiling was low, very low, and there were thick wooden pillars from floor to ceiling, and around those pillars were women, as loud and as riotous as the men.

" 'Will you be having a drink, Tom?' George asked when I came alongside.

" 'Yes,' I said, looking around the club. 'I'll have one of whatever it is you're drinking there.'

"As it happened, that was rye whisky, from Canada. And when I drank that first drink it seemed I took all the harshness of the talk and the smoke and the piano noise and the laughter, I swallowed it all down with the whisky.

"So there we stood and drank some more.

"I tried to tell George what I was working on, but gave it up for I was scanning, scanning, the club. The bright spots; the young women. It was too noisy for talk anyway.

"I took a stool at the bar.

"And by now I was finding all congenial and I studied my arm, y'know, there on the bar holding another glass of the rye whisky. I studied that arm as if it were somebody else's arm, and I lifted that arm and down the whisky went. George and the others made sure my glass was never empty for long. They all seemed to be having great fun watching me drink.

"This might have been the first time I'd had a drink in a long time, you see. It is possible. Certainly it was the first time in a long while I'd felt either bit drunk. I chuckled to myself when I made the connection between the good and warm and comfortable feelings I was feeling and the rye whisky I was consuming. After all the work I'd done, I wanted to feel a good feeling. I deserved that.

"I closed my eyes, and when I opened them I had to squint. The light in that club was hard and in orientation the place seemed to be at a tilt to me. I looked around but could see George nowhere. Kerrywinkle's was foreign to me again.

"Alone, I remember thinking. I could not move and I imagined Madeline there before me, as she'd been that night when we danced, and I would not let that image go.

"All the good fortune that seemed to be hers in marrying into that great merchant family . . . I shook my head in disbelief when I heard they'd driven her out. Driven out for letting it be known that Wes Woolfrey was both wife-beater and philanderer. I told George to help her out any way we could.

"Those were my thoughts that night and then some smooth, silken movement directed to me roused me back to the noise and the smoke. A woman moved towards me, full and fluidly. All the while I'd been thinking of Madeline I'd been staring at her, her hair a tangle of loose brown curls, and lips so red with a knowing twist that might have been a smile and her shoulders showing white and vulnerable, sloping into deep softness and straight towards me she walked. We talked a time, and then we left.

"Gone for the night!

"After that, it was every night, and other women, and rye whisky played a part in every one."

Tom and his party reluctantly joined the Coalition only after much discussion amongst themselves and serious consultation with their constituents about conscription. In return for the relative political peace of Coalition, Tom was appointed Minister of Fisheries. More importantly, there were guarantees from both other parties that, should the war last longer than expected, there'd be no conscription without a referendum. These guarantees were demanded by the people of the FC districts, now generally referred to as the Collective Coast, in return for their endorsement of the Coalition. The Collective Coast was in as much patriotic fervour as any other part of the country, but the harvesting of the fish was the work of fathers and sons, and no one wanted their fate in the hands of those who did not understand or care about that.

Thus the compact was made between people and politicians, with Tom the guarantor.

Disputes between parties continued to be regular features of government, but under Coalition the wheels set in motion to win the war turned smoothly and in the spirit of judicious cooperation the government continued to pass one landmark piece of legislation after another.

At official functions Tom always found time to stand shoulder-to-shoulder with Hammond, whom he continued to treat as a confidant and Tom always supplied him with one quote that he'd give no other. For this reason the *Mail* wanted Hammond there on those occasions.

Hammond saw the gradual unofficial changes as well. In Tom's hand a glass of whisky, first sometimes, then always. And later a merry-go-round of women on his arm.

"That last year of war, that was a troubled time. I'm sure we did our work in government and accomplished many things, but I'd not be able to give particulars because for me there was no other issue but conscription.

"There were arguments for and against. In the papers and on the streets. And the debate in the Legislature could sometimes get as heated as it did everywhere else. Truth be told, though, in the House the heat had no centre, and *I* was responsible for that because *I* spoke neither 'for' nor 'against.'

"We had promised: *No conscription without referendum* and if we held true to that position now, with the Conscription Act before us, the government had to fall. My people wanted me to do that, to vote against, to topple the government. I was doubtful. I was not as sure as I thought I would always be as to the right thing to do, so I kept silent, and confided my innermost thoughts to no one.

"The Speaker adjourned the Legislature for a week to give us time to consult both conscience and constituents.

"I took his charge seriously.

"I wore a long loose overcoat, collar up, a shapeless thing so as not to be recognized. Everything I needed in a leather valise. And made it to the station just in time.

"Found my compartment, shut the door and slumped in the seat.

"Now this is the way it was:

"The window was open about half an inch. The night air whistled in. The noise of the train, too. I'd had a couple of drinks by then. Maybe half a bottle of rye whisky.

"It was freezing in that compartment. I kept my gloves on. Took a drink.

"Pulled the heavy curtain across, hooked it down, then stood unsteadily in the centre of the compartment and was having a long drink to finish that bottle when the train lurched, and when I reached for a handhold I fell to the bed.

"My mouth, throat and stomach were all in a burn by then. All else was cold to the bones. I pulled blankets out of their tuck, and wrapped them around. My stomach was heaving, bile in my mouth. I fell asleep or passed out.

"When I awoke the train was still moving, and my mouth had an evil taste. You can imagine.

"From my valise, I took out a new bottle, sat on the edge of the bed there and had a couple of drinks.

"I'd learned by then to be a clever drunk, y'know. I tried, always, never to look drunk. So before I changed trains, I turned up the lamp, washed, shaved, had another drink, and brushed my teeth.

"I was the only one to step down from the train. I walked in on one side of the station, straight through to an exit on the other side onto another platform where the pride of the FC Railroad, my own *FC Flyer*, was waiting for me.

"I remember the conductor was a young man. He walked with a limp and used a cane. He stepped forward as if to challenge a stranger, but recognized me then and tipped his cap.

"I walked to my own coach. Warm inside that one, and quiet, spacious and well lit, light reflecting off brass and glass, just the way I'd wanted it.

"Now out on the platform the conductor was speaking to the

engineer. The engineer had a withered arm. Watching them through my window I could not take my eyes off that useless limb.

"You know, I once stood in the House and demanded compensation and the creation of opportunities for those injured at work. The hoots and howls were fierce. 'Who will hire broken men?' they shouted. 'I will!' I shouted back ... and I did. Many jobs in Union Cove were held by men who'd been injured at work. Some were blind, others had broken bones, what-have-you, and they'd never expected to work again. But we were building and expanding and hiring and we made it our policy that work would be found, or made, for any such man if the man wanted to work.

"And men who'd long ago given up hope of getting anything better out of life made appeals and we found jobs for them in the store or in the office and we paid them regular wages. And harder workers or better employees are not to be found anywhere in the country.

"George says I peopled Union Cove with those I brought back from the dead.

"On that night, though, the lame and injured ... they seemed too great a burden. More than I could bear. I felt as broken as any of them.

"The train pulled slowly out of the station. I lay my head back on the seat, closed my eyes."

4

On one wall of the studio hung framed photographs of Tom, smiling, formally shaking hands with representatives of the Fishermen's Collective, with politicians and dignitaries from home and abroad. The most interesting picture, the one holding pride of place on this wall, was of Tom and a black man wearing a skullcap made of animal fur.

In order to appear together, in closeup, they'd tilted their heads until they'd touched, and where Tom's left forehead contacted the black man's right, they seemed, through some anomaly of light, to be not just touching, but joined.

They look out from the picture joyously.

The man's name was M'Papa. He was West Indian. Rare though it was to see a black man on the streets of St. John's, it was even more astonishing that M'Papa was the trusted agent of a *white* fish broker, and that he'd come to Newfoundland with full responsibility and authority to conduct business as he saw fit with Tom Vincent. Tom and the Fishermen's Collective were well-known to Caribbean toilers, M'Papa had reported. Their reputation for fair dealing had carried that far south, and further, on the salt-fish schooners.

When Prime Minister Caines heard that M'Papa was in Newfoundland to negotiate with Tom as President of the FC, *not* as Minister of Fisheries, he unleashed such an attack against Tom, first in the House and later in the newspapers, that even the longest serving Members of the House of Assembly, those most used to Caines' brand of vitriol, were surprised.

When Caines first rose in the House to speak to the issue, the chamber fell strangely, expectantly, quiet. With a nod to the Chair, Caines pointed to Tom and began. "Mr. Speaker, the Honourable

Member from Our Island has been quick in the past to condemn the corrupt practices of Members of this House. He is quick to set himself up as a man of good intention, a man with the interests of the working man closest to his heart. Still, Mr. Speaker, he remains President of his precious Fishermen's Collective even as he sits as a Member of this House. You can be sure, Mr. Speaker, he would be the first to note the conflict if it were some other Member's situation."

The Prime Minister's small body trembled. He turned away from Tom, and in short jerky movements poured himself a glass of water, spilling some. He put a hand on a hip, raised the glass to his lips and drank very slowly, fully aware that he had the House's undivided attention as he had not had it for some time.

He returned the glass to the table with a loud echoing *thok!* startling some Members.

"Mr. Speaker, when Mr. M'Papa comes to this country to do business with the Government, the Minister of Fisheries forgets his obligations and duties to the people. He tries instead to do a dirty deal between his own union enterprises and the interests Mr. M'Papa represents. The people are outraged, Mr. Speaker, for we have all seen the Honourable Member badger men out of office for less."

When Tom rose, he admitted that the Prime Minister would indeed be right to be indignant if what he said were true. The facts, however, spoke for themselves. In the first place, M'Papa had not come to St. John's to do business with government, but with the FC, because the FC, unlike the government agency or the independent houses, guaranteed both price *and* quality of fish. And secondly, Tom continued, he was fully aware of the proprieties of the situation and had already directed Mr. M'Papa to the Fisheries Department.

This was not, in fact, the truth at that moment, but George, listening and watching in the Strangers' Gallery, played the good lieutenant well. He quietly left the gallery and before the House had adjourned that day, M'Papa *had* been referred to the Fisheries Department.

At the union offices on Water Street West the reception to welcome

M'Papa rose quickly, light as a balloon, to a crescendo in talk and laughter and clinking glasses, then was just as quickly exhausted, leaving Tom and George and a few others of the inner circle sitting comfortably with M'Papa. Ties and jackets loose, the table covered with empty glasses.

M'Papa raised his glass and drank to Tom's health, then Pike interrupted everything for several minutes, setting up his camera and taking the picture that would document the only meeting between these two. Then it was quiet a moment and M'Papa looked around, everyone waiting for him to speak. He sat on the edge of his chair, hands squeezed between his knees.

"Okay, okay," M'Papa began. "I will tell you a story."

M'Papa told them his island was as different as different could be from Newfoundland.

His land, he said, was so very hot, and thick with trees of all kinds and flowers of all colours, and there were white beaches where the sand was too hot to walk, and the water warm enough to soothe most aching bones.

In Newfoundland, he said, you have the hard gray rock. On his island, he said, it was coral pink and red that made hills and valleys.

In Newfoundland he had noticed everyone was white, but on his island there was the white and the black. And in Newfoundland it seemed to him that it was the rich keeping the poor fisherman down. So it had been for a very long time on his island, where there was the white and the poor black.

There was one high hill that ran the whole length of the island. Too steep to climb, trees too thick to slash through, you walk around it if you want to get to the other side. But this was not to the liking of the white, so he called the engineer and the engineer went up and down the island carrying his transit in a square wooden box. All up and down the island and all over the hill, he set up his transit and took angles, bearings and levels. And when that job was done, the white sent hundreds of black labourers to the place where the engineer said, and a strip of trees was slashed and cut and burned, up the hill, down the hill. Some died there from the snakebite, but the white did not meddle in their death affairs — best to let them take care of their own, they said. Then the soil was scraped from the coral and buckets filled with that soil were carried down the hill by men two at a time, and men broke arms and legs and backs. A few tumbled to death.

Then to work on the coral with rock saws, and so began days of great anguish in the sun. They sawed through coral, backs bent naked to the sun. The air was a hot mist of pink sawdust that stuck to the sweaty bodies, caked up in nostrils, and coated throats and lungs. From their lungs they hacked plugs of phlegm, pink and red.

The rock saws were long and broad with heavy wooden handles, each end needing two men to rip the blade through the coral. Over two years, many men died from heat exhaustion.

The coral was nicked, then notched, then squared, and then the rest of the hill was sawed out in blocks, block by block, until you could walk from one side of the island to the other through a sheer pink-walled pass.

When the work was done, the white held a party in the middle of the pass. The workers there served finger sandwiches and poured drinks for invited guests.

"So, Tom Vincent," M'Papa said, "you see in different times and places and in different ways things are much the same. Some people do not want other people to rise above their station. You keep a people in a place long enough and they believe that is where they belong. Until there is someone to help them recognize and to re-claim their power. In Newfoundland you have not lately had to fight the gun and the whip, but from what I know of you, Tom Vincent, I believe you see your brother in the black."

They were all silent.

"So," M'Papa finished quietly, "I'll visit your Department of Fisheries, because you have asked me to, but, when that is done, I will decide to do my business with the FC!"

The night went down on a roll and roar of laughter.

But no one laughed when later they heard M'Papa's own people had long harboured some grievance against him, and one dark night he was spirited away, for good.

5

I woke up, went directly from the train to the ferry where I chose to sit alone on deck. On Our Island, the FC buildings stood out in dark silhouette against a dark sky.

"I made sure I had my valise before I stepped off the ferry and trudged home. The salt sea air did me some good. Cleared my head as it hadn't been cleared for some time, and though a great weariness still dragged on me, I saw everything clearly, just for a moment. The edge of that perception cut me to the quick of my being.

"Conscription. That was the issue. And, you see, in that moment my thoughts were free and clean and true but I did *not* want the whole picture.

"I imagined the Speaker of the House: '*Mr. Vincent*,' he'd say, '*on the Bill of Conscription before the House, your vote please?*' "

" 'No,' he'd be expecting me to say. Because I'd promised all I would vote against. They'd be as sure and certain of my vote as they'd be wrong.

"Let me tell you about the mighty issue of conscription:

"War came, the Empire called, the young men answered. I visited all the FC districts and spoke to the young men. Join the fight for King and Country!

"I felt nervous only the first time I gave that speech. That was on Our Island in Union Hall, decked out in flags and hung with huge posters and in the back corner a small desk, and two army officers in full regalia.

"A union crowd, for sure. I felt the buzz of excitement, the anticipation in the Hall. When I stood to speak, there was applause and all that, and when I'd quieted them down, I cleared my throat, and for a moment did not know what to say. Looked left and right, then down, in thought, searching for the right words, and the longer I waited, the more important those first words became.

" 'We are in danger,' I said finally, 'of losing everything we have worked for.' And I realized as I spoke I was like a piano player learning a new tune. The people knew the great unionist, and now I gave them the ardent patriot, and as closely as they listened, I just as closely noted their reaction to what I said, and how I said it, so that by the time I closed that speech, I knew all there was to know about the tune to play to get the volunteers out.

"Then this strange thing: the entire assembly stood as one to applaud, to stamp their feet and to cheer, but as suddenly as the roar had gone up so now it was reduced to a single note, a scream: sitting rigid in her chair, head thrown back, mouth wide open, a thin woman all in black, white hair drawn back severely into a bun. Her wail had pierced and deflated the roar, filled all the sound and space that was given over to it.

"A handsome young man but for a chin all scarred was holding her arm, gently but firmly shaking it, trying to calm her. 'Mother! Mother!' he whispered repeatedly, his face equal parts of concern and embarrassment, but she ignored him and howled us all into silence.

"When she stopped, she directed a look towards me that I shall never forget. George said I took a step back as he'd never seen me give way before any man.

"The young man said, 'I'm sorry about this, sir. Mother has been crazy with grief since Father died.'

" '*You will pay if you take my son!*' she shouted at me, half rising out of her seat. She had not taken her eyes off me. Her son gently cooed her back to sitting. And then the strength seemed to go from her. Her eyes clouded, her head fell sideways.

" 'You'll forgive her, sir?' the young man said.

"I said, 'A son who keeps and helps his mother is a good man, and a brave man, too. There's no shame in it.'

" 'Thank you, sir,' the young man said. He helped his mother to her feet. Diminished by grief. 'I'll be signing on soon as I can,' he said to me over his shoulder as he led her away. There was a smatter of applause, then the hall exploded with cheers, deafening as thunder, or cannon fire."

" 'They'll volunteer because of what I've said and how I've said it,' I told George later. 'Some of them will be killed. Some of them are sure to die. It's a powerful gift to be able to move people so.'

"The Collective Coast was proud to have it recorded that it sent a fair share of young men out to fight the war.

"But how that war dragged on: a second, unbelievably, a third year, and bad news from the trenches too. In that battle of the Somme, our poor boys slaughtered! From all fronts in Europe, urgent calls were still coming for replacements. Then Prime Minister Caines without any consultation at all, and against his word to me, introduced a bill to conscript. There was no mention of the referendum promised when we'd formed the Coalition. *That* is the way of the world."

"Inside my bungalow down in Union Cove, I was thinking on all this, and at the same time trying not to think on it at all. I tried to turn up the lights but the power had already been shut down for the night. In the kitchen I groped against the wall until I found the master switch. When I pulled it down, blue sparks jumped between switches and blades. Through the window I saw the street lamps all at once dimly light up, then flutter their way to brightness. The dark houses looked surprised by the light. Then light suddenly shone in the windows of the bakery and the cooperage, the coal storage shed and Union Hall. And down on the wharves the lights came on in stepwise pairs as if, I fancied, treading water. Those businesses, that light — great triumphs, but never had I been so *un*moved by those sights as I was that night.

"I pulled the switch, plunged the cove back to darkness. Could feel a hush descend on everything.

"I found the house switch and pulled that smaller one down. The electricity crackled throughout, and I was pleased. It was heat, not light, that I needed.

"Later I woke up trying to get my breath. Tried to loosen my collar. The suffocating heat in that room was like a pair of pliers pinching the bridge of my nose.

"I stumbled to the door, threw it open, and the pre-dawn night was waiting there on a cool breeze.

"No comfort for the broken in the land of the broken, was a thought that came to me then.

"Before light, I was headed back to town, to St. John's.

"I felt between everything.

"You see I had a vision for the FC and now we were in government and had been battling for the things we wanted, and much of what we wanted had come to pass because of the Coalition, because I'd become the Minister of Fisheries.

"I stood against conscription, but now, if I voted against the bill to conscript, the government would fail, simple as that. And the FC's power, and my own ministry, too, it would all go down. So to vote against the bill would be political suicide for the FC. After all the hard work and sacrifice, it was too soon, it was just too soon, to let it all go. And at the centre, I cannot say 'at the heart,' I could prevent it from happening though it would appear I was *acting against* those who had chosen me to *act for* them.

"A 'Yes' vote was a vote against my own people, but it would uphold the government and preserve our power. It would be for their own ultimate good. Should I do this one thing against them in order to help them? I did not know then. That was my problem. The way of the world. I did not move for some time.

"I needed to drink."

6

Pike pushes his bottle of rye whisky aside, stands up, and goes once again to check the camera that has been set, ready and waiting for over an hour. He is hazed by the whisky, but as soon as he touches his camera, he begins to work soberly and efficiently. He minutely adjusts the height of a tripod leg, leans over the camera and looks down into the eyepiece. He pulls a measuring tape from his vest pocket, hooks it to the camera, steps into the hot glare of the centred and reflected light. He walks off the distance from the camera to the focus of the light, the empty chair where Tom will sit, as he has sat many times before, for the record, on the eve or on the day of all major votes in the House of Assembly. Pictures of Tom are everywhere about the shop. Today's picture will commemorate his vote on the Conscription Act.

Pike scans the backdrop of dark heavy curtains. Satisfied with his preparation, he unhooks the tape, stands there absentmindedly in the heat and light winding it up.

The long silence upstairs bursts into a loud shouting for two voices. He looks up, hears words — 'whisky,' 'Collective,' and 'Conscription,' all in a jumble. Then as quickly as it was broken, silence is restored.

Upstairs George now quietly asks, pleads with, Tom to lay off the booze, but Tom, half-naked, fresh out of a bath and dripping water on the hardwood floors, defiantly pours himself a double shot of whisky, drinks it down. George says nothing.

"Why," Tom asks, "did you bring this up again? We've talked about this before."

George says, "It's getting worse."

"Go way with you!"

"It's no good to talk to you."

"Not a bit, George b'y, not a bit. Drink?"

Pike lowers his eyes from the ceiling, his baldness a sheen of perspiration. He tucks the tape into his vest pocket, goes to his bottle, pours himself another drink, sits down and waits.

When Tom enters he is wearing a very fine, very expensive charcoal-gray suit. In his hand he carries a matching fedora which he drops on the table.

The Speaker is canvassing the front row when Hammond squeezes in alongside George in the crowded Strangers' Gallery.

The politicians stand, nod, sit down.

"How are they voting?"

"No surprises at all," George whispers. "All as expected."

Soon enough it comes around to the FC, Tom first. As always, all other FC members will follow his lead.

Tom looks up. Stands.

"Could I hear the motion please? I believe that's allowed."

The Speaker nods and Tom sits while the Recording Officer stands and reads the motion in a loud voice. No one, not even Tom, seems to be listening.

Tom stands again, and for a moment he is unable to speak.

"Well I'll be damned!" Hammond hears George say under his breath.

The Speaker: Mr. Vincent, your vote, please.

Mr. Vincent: Aye.

"After the vote, without a word to anyone, I went back to my office there in the building and locked the door behind me. Only a moment later they were knocking and shouting questions.

"I was planning to wait until they were all gone. Then I would leave.

"For the second time in my life, I thought of a great wheel. Later on through the window, watching the sun fall behind trees, a beam struck my eyes and I imagined the sun arcing over the earth, imagined the curve of a great wheel that I'd once taken on the rise, now descending.

"I dropped an empty bottle to the floor. Pushed myself up out of a chair. Had trouble keeping my balance: had to stop and steady myself several times.

"Before I unlocked the door, the world slipped out from beneath my feet again. Then I was steady again. Opened the door wide.

"George was there, and next to George a man I recognized as a doctor, and next to the doctor, Madeline Woolfrey.

"George asked, 'Do you know what you've done? Do you know what happened in the House there?'

"I nodded.

"George said, 'We've got to get you off the liquor, Tom boy. The doctor's here to help.'

"I don't know why, perhaps it was because Madeline was there, or because I had no energy left to expend on anything anymore, or because I was just altogether too drunk, but I didn't resist.

"The doctor ordered me to lie down on the couch and after the examination I remember him saying that I would need close watching if I were to come off the booze.

"George took an armful of bottles from the liquor cabinet. That was the last I saw of them.

"Madeline placed a washcloth on my forehead and I opened my eyes, and for a moment I stared at her. Then she left the room, but I remembered exactly the points where our bodies had touched: as she applied the cloth: the press of her fingers through the cloth against my temples, her hip solidly pressing into my own as she sat on the edge of the couch.

"Then she was back, standing behind the couch, and I aware of her then, and aware ever after of wherever she was whenever she moved.

"Then George came back.

" 'You've been drinking too bloody much,' George said.

"I nodded towards Madeline. 'What about . . . ?' I asked.

"George said, 'You know who she is, Tom,' and that's all I remember of that. Fell asleep, I guess. Or passed out, more likely."

PART VI

*T*here is no end to his need, Madeline often thought during Tom's long recuperation down in Pike's Lane.

The doors were locked, the world carried on its business without them. Tom took to a narrow bed beneath a window. Madeline opened it for him when he ran fevers, closed it when he had shivering fits. She calmed him when he awoke from his terrors, stayed with him always when he was awake.

He went unshaven and lost weight because he could not eat. He did not want to. For a day and a night, and then another day, he vomited: a yellow mucus at first, then a thick, clear bile. When his stomach was empty, he had the dry heaves until the muscles around his midriff were so sore that it hurt even to draw breath. Vomitus clung in dry bits to his hair and whiskers and stained both bed shirts and bed sheets. He was foul smelling, but would not allow Madeline near enough to clean him.

At times, to Madeline, he did not even look to be of the same world as everyone else. He weakly struck out at her when she approached, but she soon managed to settle him. She got him to sit on the edge of the bed, and then tried to spoon rabbit soup into him, only to have most of it spewed back in her face.

In his daily delirium he wondered why she was there, and looked at her lethally, as if she might be just another unreality thrown up by his mind. Then he would look about as if all were foreign to him. Sometimes he awoke from fitful sleep screaming out her name or screaming for rabbit soup and as often as not he'd sink right back to the depths from which he'd momentarily risen.

He began to behave childishly, expecting Madeline to be near when he woke and to stay close by. He would whine when she left the room. So she dealt with him as if he *were* a child, reassuring him that she would be nearby, promising to look in on him often, keeping that promise.

One night she decided to take a bath, wash her hair, and change into clean clothes. She left him alone to make her preparations.

Her apron wrap was soiled and stained, her undergarments chafed in some places and stuck to her in others. Yesterday she had piled her hair on top of her head. It was so matted that she did not want it falling around her face. Now it was tangled as well. A stiffness in her lower back made her wince.

Though George Gill had patiently taught her how to use the alternate system of electric light and heat, Madeline chose for simplicity's sake to use only the woodstove and the kerosene lanterns. In the kitchen she started a good strong fire in the woodstove. Then, in the pantry off the kitchen, she used the water faucet. Unlike the electrical systems, this convenient gravity-based water supply, as George had described it, was simple to use. She put the boilers under the tap, turned the handle. The water right away flowed steadily and evenly. When the boilers were full, she turned the valve off and carried them out to the stove.

The room was warming up nicely. Madeline fed the fire another stick of wood.

From her own room she brought out towels, a wash basin and jug, soaps and combs, a small brown bag of baking soda, a tooth-brush and a shaving mirror, and clean clothes. From the bathing room next to her room she pulled out a white wooden tub. It was heavier and larger than she'd expected, so she folded a towel to put under one end of it. Lifting the other end off the floor, she dragged the tub into the kitchen, not without back pain.

The kitchen was warmer still, wood crackling in the stove. The sides of the boilers were warm to the touch. After several trips from pantry to kitchen carrying a small pot filled with water, she had a good base of cold water in the tub.

The kitchen curtains had been pulled across. Only the door to Tom's office was open.

Realizing she'd forgotten to check on him, as promised, she hurried to his room. Facing the wall, he was soundly and peacefully asleep. He took breath deeply and evenly; there was no twitching or turning. She watched longer than she needed to, and when she was doubly sure he was in no distress, she left the room, quietly closing the door behind her.

Then she went to close the office door. Just inside the dark office, there was a chair, and a book resting on the arm of the chair caught her eye. She picked it up and leaned sideways so she could study it in the light coming from the kitchen. It was an old book, much of the lettering on the spine worn away. *A Handbook To The Stars And Planets.* She opened it, flipped through the pages randomly. Many diagrams and tables that she did not understand. The pages were crisp and clean except for notes written here and there in neat handwriting on blank pages provided for one's own observations. The book, Madeline realized, was not so much old as well-used. After putting it back where she found it, she closed the door on her way out.

She placed a chair from the kitchen table near the white tub. She undid the neck and waist ties of her apron wrap. As soon as the apron was loose, it fell to her feet. She stepped out of it, kicked it aside. She stretched her neck as she undid the top button of her blouse, then she undid the buttons all the way down but did not take the blouse off. She undid the hooks of her corset from top to bottom and this was a relief. Then, with blouse and corset hanging loose and open, she sat down.

Looking at Tom's oversized washtub she remembered the first time she'd walked into the bathing room in Woolfrey House.

It was a high-ceilinged room brightly painted, white with lemon wainscotting. There was a large window with square panes of bevelled glass, most frosted but some coloured. On each wall was a smiling porcelain cherub, looking as if he had just that moment leaned into the room. Each of the identical curly-headed fellows held a gas lamp high in an upraised hand. The lamps had burned so brightly that first day there was no shadow in the room at all.

The centrepiece of the bathing room was the 'New York Steamer' — a white tub that in shape resembled nothing so much as a large teacup with a canopy. The canopy could be raised and lowered and, when raised, created its own steam. The inside surface of the Steamer was smooth and cool to the touch, but on that first day the tub was already filled for her. She stepped into it with high hopes, but the Steamer did not live up to its promises. Water did not long hold heat in it, and when the canopy was raised, no cloud of steam formed like that engulfing the head of the young lady pictured in the literature. At best a few drops of tepid water dripped from the canopy. Each time Madeline used the Steamer to bathe, she was hopeful it would perform as described, and each time she was disappointed. There was no trick to it, the maid servants confirmed. It simply did not work.

Madeline pulled the corset out from under her blouse, then lifted and laid the hems of both skirt and slip on her knees. Still sitting, she bent from the waist, unlaced her black shoes, and pulled them off. She wiggled her toes. She rolled one stocking down and off, then the other. On both legs the tight tops of her shoes had left deep red marks and here and there red indentations held the pattern of her knitted socks. She stood, slipped her thumbs under the waistbands of both skirt and slip, and wiggled them down to her ankles. These, along with her blouse, she added to the growing bundle of clothes.

She stood naked now except for the long loose underwear that covered her completely from waist to knee.

She reached up with both hands to unpin her hair, so tangled that it was hard to get her fingers through it. But untangled it must be, and even though she forced her fingers through cautiously, her hand sometimes slipped and pulled at her scalp painfully. Tears came to her eyes.

One day, in the well-lit bathing room of Woolfrey House, Wes had savagely knocked her to the floor. Then he had crouched down next to her. She was naked and crying, her nose bleeding. He bunched her hair in his fist and pulled as if he were trying to lift her off the floor. The pain took her breath away.

"Honour and obey!" he had shouted into her ear. "Honour and obey! Do you not remember your vows?"

Madeline grabbed his wrist with both hands, trying to pull him away, but he clenched his fist tighter in her hair.

"Stop . . ." she pleaded. "Please!" With a final tug, he loosened his grip, pushed her head away. She sobbed, great tears running down her face, splashing onto the floor, and great drops of blood from her nose splashing there too.

Wes stood up, brushed some of her hair from his hand.

"Honour and obey," he said flatly.

"I promised," Madeline said between sobs, her shoulders heaving, "to honour and obey under love" — she looked over her shoulder at him — "not under this terror!"

"Terror?" Wes scoffed. "This is nothing. If you ever again speak to anyone of our private life" — and remembering what had sparked his anger, he raised a fist as if to hit her again. She cowered, and he waved dismissively, disgustedly, then turned and walked out.

Now, sitting in Tom Vincent's kitchen waiting for her bath water to heat, she had all the knots and tangles out of her hair and was easily pulling a comb through it. A tear ran down her cheek. She had few tears left for what might have been. She flicked the tear away with her finger.

Regardless of how Wes treated her, however, she would not, could not, be silent — to do so, she knew, would be her ruin. She told the servants. They did not want to know. She told Tobias and Sophie. They acknowledged it not at all. Tobias simply called for their coats and hats and very politely they took their leave.

Madeline washed her hair at the kitchen table using jug and basin and more water than she thought she'd need. Only on a second washing did the soap foam in her hair, and only on the third rinsing did she feel her hair had at last come clean.

She threw the dirtied water out the window. The first time she covered herself with a towel before opening the curtain and lifting the window, but after that she did not bother. It was late and it seemed she had the night to herself. After discarding the last water, naked to the waist, she poked her towel-turbaned head and shoulders fully out of the window and looked down Pike's Lane. Not a light was showing in any of the houses, but the moon was full and the night cloudless. So quiet and peaceful.

She always liked the feel of cool night air on her body. She glanced up at the stars, thought of Tom's book. What of that sky might he read and record, she wondered. She did not even know what time of the night it was, and strangely, but strongly for a moment, that thought made her feel light enough to float out through the window and away. She was still smiling when she pulled her head back in, pushed the window down and closed the curtain.

The water was ready.

When she finished filling the tub, the water at just the right temperature, she took off her bloomers and carefully climbed in. It was pure pleasure as she felt the water cover her body. She moaned a little.

She liked the size and shape of the tub and the height of the water around her as she lay back, the tub almost long enough to stretch her legs straight out, the hot water covering her chest, the heat loosening and lengthening all her muscles. She could not resist; she closed her eyes.

One night in a rage over something or other (there was *always* something or other) Wes had locked her in her room.

The door opened next morning when she tried it, but she was alone in the house except for servants. And alone she remained for over a week, with no knowledge of where her husband was. She put her worry out of her head by focusing on her accounting.

Then one morning she glanced out her bedroom window to see an austere looking man, a stranger, walking up the path. In his hand he carried a thin leather document case. She wondered who he might be, sat in her chair and waited. Before long there was a soft knock on her door.

"Come in," Madeline said.

A young maid entered, an open envelope and letter in her hand.

"A Mr. Watts wishes to speak with you." The girl handed over envelope and letter. "He has a letter of introduction from Wesley. It all seems in order."

Madeline needed only a glance at the letter — "will introduce Leander Watts" — to verify Wes's signature. Then she handed it back, her heart pounding as she stood up.

"The purpose of his visit?"

"He would not say. Just that he must speak with you."

Madeline nodded. "Tell him I will be down directly. Have him wait in the room where I work on the accounts." Where, she thought, I will feel most comfortable.

The girl nodded and withdrew.

Madeline closed her eyes, and put her hand over her heart. When it was beating normally and her mind was calm, she went downstairs.

No matter how often she thought about that meeting, there was much she could not remember of it. It was as if the message Leander Watts delivered erased from her memory all the lesser details of their encounter.

Mr. Watts was perfectly courteous in every respect but his gauntness communicated menace. His hair was gray and straight, combed to one side. His limbs were lank and long.

A quarter of an hour after they met she knew only what he wanted her to know about himself. Had there been vague talk of the weather? His trip by rail and boat from St. John's? He was a friend of the Woolfreys. He was making this visit at their request. He did not convey personal greetings. Given his obvious sense of propriety, she knew it was not a case of forgetfulness.

Madeline sat behind her desk, hands on her lap, her face deliberately composed. She gave Mr. Watts her fullest attention.

By the time the second quarter hour had passed, Madeline would have guessed him to be a man of God, or a member of the government, and she could plainly see that he was observing her as closely as she was him.

By carefully chosen reference to certain events — blood on the bathing room floor was one — Madeline knew that Mr. Watts had full and intimate knowledge of her life as Wes's wife. He reminded her of her wifely vows and duties then watched her reaction, a slight dismissive shrug of her shoulder. Mr. Watts said nothing, as if her response was exactly as predicted.

Moments later, sounding as if he knew something she did not, he turned the conversation to the matter of her upcoming teacher registration. He seemed to be suggesting she might encounter some difficulty this time. In the past, registration had been a matter of the most routine sort. Her anger rose to think that someone would make this difficult for her, but she kept it from showing.

For the third quarter of an hour Mr. Watts spoke like a physician. He talked about the Asylum —

In the tub in Tom's kitchen, Madeline's heart beat faster in recall than it had beat at the time. She had not recognized her peril then.

Mr. Watts said he knew all about the Asylum. He knew women there, young and every bit as attractive as Madeline, incarcerated for 'Marital Recalcitrance.'

At the time Madeline thought such issues were irrelevant, so she did not react.

For the remaining quarter of that hour, Madeline knew Mr. Watts for what he was, a lawyer. He helped her to understand that the Woolfrey family would not return to Woolfrey House as long as she was there. When she understood that he was talking about divorce, she closed her eyes, looked deeply inward and told herself she would maintain her composure. Mr. Watts noted her response, stopped speaking. When she opened her eyes again, he smiled a little, raised his eyebrows in question and, when she nodded, he continued on.

The air was warmly scented from the vanilla soap, and the water was still warm when she stepped out. From the warmer on the stove she took her towels. She draped one around her shoulders like a shawl. Setting one foot on the chair, she began to dry herself with the other towel.

The second hour with Mr. Watts had been all negotiation. Her only weapon had been the Woolfreys' ardent desire to avoid, at any cost, the embarrassment of a public scandal because of Wes's philandering and assaultive ways. In the end she signed documents which guaranteed that in due course she would receive an income, which Mr. Watts described as "a very generous allowance." Until such time as the dissolution of her union with Wes Woolfrey was finalized, she could, if she wished, live in any one of the Woolfrey homes except Woolfrey House itself. She chose the St. John's residence on Circular Road.

One day, months after moving to St. John's, she encountered George Gill. She complained of finding the time on her hands dreadfully long, George asked if she would be interested in working for the FC. When she mentioned her accounting experience, he was delighted. A few days later she had more than enough accounting to keep her mind occupied. When George next came to see her, it was to ask her to take care of Tom.

Clean and warm in her night dress now, Madeline unwrapped the towel from her hair and combed it out silky smooth.

She sat at the kitchen table and set up a rectangular two-sided shaving mirror. One side reflected her normally; the other magnified everything. It was this she now used to examine and clean her teeth. As she had been taught many years ago, she opened her mouth wide and examined each tooth, as best she could, for stains. Her examination was thorough and methodical. She had long grown used to the gross and magnified distortions of her mouth in the mirror. When she discovered a discoloration, she scraped at it lightly with a small metal instrument that resembled a flat-headed screwdriver.

When she was done, she gave her teeth a vigorous brushing with baking soda and water, and made one final check in the magnifying mirror. In the other side of the mirror she saw herself normal, and was not unhappy with the woman who looked back.

But a weariness was on her now. She'd had a notion to put everything back in order before going to bed, but she knew she had to let it go. There would be time tomorrow. She took a lantern to her bedroom and laid it on the night table. Sitting on the edge of the bed, she blew the lamp out, swung her legs into bed and settled comfortably down. The pain in her back was gone.

The next day Tom let Madeline wash him as he lay in bed. He kept his eyes closed, fell in and out of sleep.

The following morning he woke calm and alert, and sent for George.

"Madeline says you're too weak to work," George said as he entered the room, "and before you say anything, *I'm* telling you there's nothing for you to worry about. The FC is doing business-as-usual, and all our men in the House are going to watch over Fisheries. If anything comes up that they can't manage, they're going to bring it to me so I can bring it to you. So far though, no problems."

"That's fine," Tom said, propping himself up on an elbow, "but I have legislation ready to go."

"Done."

"Done?"

"Last week." George pulled up a chair and sat near the head of the bed.

"As quick as that?"

George shrugged. "Well, yes, but not as quick as you think. You've missed a few weeks here."

"Oh, right, weeks," Tom said. "Weeks?"

George nodded.

Tom lay back in bed, dumbfounded. He studied the blank ceiling for a time, then, as if he suddenly remembered George was still there, he asked, "Was it hard to push through? Did they change much of it?"

George shook his head. "They haven't tried to block anything since the vote."

Tom turned, looked at George. "And what about that? Conscription, I mean?"

George nodded. "Caines scrabbled together some kind of a plan. He called up sixty-seven fellows right away, from all over. Since then, as far as I can see, they've done more parading on the front pages with Caines than they have on the training field. They'll soon be going overseas, Caines says." Then he fell silent, hands on his knees, thoughtful.

"What are you thinking?" Tom asked.

"That he'll send them," George said, "ready or not."

A few days later Tom asked Madeline to sing for him and she did, soft and low.

He spoke of their dance.

Her voice and his great long bouts of sleep soon had him hungering for other things.

One day he got up and shaved himself. That same day George told him the conscripts had embarked for Europe.

It was late September.

In the pantry, Tom and Madeline stood helping each other out at close quarters, and suddenly, passionately close, a kiss, the potatoes falling, bouncing and rolling away.

That day spent in lovemaking.

His playfulness and his need a surprise to her. He told her she was delicious. She declared him fully recovered.

In the beginning what Tom wanted to capture in his poem was the early morning light as it first appeared in phantom faint lines around the window at dawn. He was always awake by then, warm and comfortable under heavy blankets with Madeline asleep next to him. At such times he felt at peace, free to follow the lazy drift of his thoughts, and he wanted his poem to convey that peace too.

For he was beginning to feel well and rested now, with a mental freshness and clarity that felt like nothing less than rebirth, and even though Madeline had by now spent many nights in his bed, he marvelled still that she had been able to bring him back.

She would be the centre of his poem. From the very first note he'd heard her sing, she'd laid claim to a certain part of his heart. But she had not had any such comparable experience that first day, not that he knew of anyway, and back then he'd feared, and then reconciled himself to the fact, that she was gone from his life, this lifetime, for good.

And now, every night . . .

George sheltered them from everything, checked on them every day, but otherwise left them to their own desires. For the first time in many years, Tom was free of all burdens and cares and responsibilities. The most important word, he thought, was *free*. It could have been a very important word in his poem, but he sensed the essence of freedom would be far beyond the reach of his poetic powers, so he would leave it out.

Half-asleep, Madeline turned to him and he responded without thinking, the most natural reflex to her motion towards him, their passion flashing from nothing to everything. To be able to write of his dissolution in the wet fires, he thought, that would be something. But he would not offend Madeline by making a poem for her that sang only of sensual delight. He was afraid she might think it low praise indeed. So he would have to leave that joyful part out too; also the window light and the peaceful feeling, for he found, after a few attempts, that he could make no headway with them at all. These restrictions in combination with Tom's own poetic inexperience might have dissuaded him altogether had he not found a focus.

One night, after lovemaking, Madeline sat on the edge of the bed, then stood, her hair falling on bare shoulders. The narrowness of her waist, the pale smooth fullness of her buttocks, the curve of her back. She turned and smiled at him, her eyes clear and bright, and he was struck in the moment by a beautiful unreality — as if time were slow, slowing, and as if everything were glowing from within. Full, alive, everything as it should be. If he died at this moment he would be assured of a sweet eternity. He watched her pull on one stocking, then the other: she was standing sideways to him, all curve and rise, her breasts trembling as, with both hands, she rolled her stocking into a loop. The soft brush of her hair. She rested her foot on the edge of the chair and, leaning forward, hair falling about her face, breast pressed against her thigh, slipped the silk stocking onto her toe, and smoothly pulled it to her knee. First one, then the other.

Simple as it was, he could not get it out of his head. It was what he wanted to capture in his poem.

But what kind of poem was it that he was writing?

When he finally set pen to paper, he found that he was using a free form, and not trying to work in stanzas or rhyme or any of that. He was glad that his mind was free to roam in a space that allowed him to think about what he really wanted to say. Since he was writing to please no one but Madeline, why should he not continue in the manner that worked best for him?

And George still kept everyone away. Tom was well-recovered from his alcoholic deliriums, not craving a drink at all, so this time was all his own, to use as he liked, an indulgence. He was required to be nowhere and to do nothing. As far as the rest of the world was concerned, his recovery was yet incomplete. So he hurried nothing, forced nothing. The days went by as if he were under some kind of spell, and day after day, page after page, in open secrecy, he worked on his poem to Madeline.

It was a great pleasure and pastime, but in the end, tongue-in-cheek, Madeline gently helped Tom accept that his talent was no match for his subject. His love poem was not so much unfinished, she suggested, as it was a work-in-progress.

Tom thought about that for a moment. Then, nodding his head, he said, "I like that . . . yes."

Eyes closed, hands laced behind his head, Tom was lying fully clothed on his bed beneath the open window and breathing deeply of the bracing tonic November air. The mid-morning quiet was broken by a yell, whether of joy or pain he could not decide before there was another, a whoop, unmistakably joyful.

Something was happening down in the lane. Tom heard doors opening, windows being raised. People began to cheer, clap and shout. One or two voices broke out in song. Sounds of commotion, sounds of celebration. Tom opened his eyes, propped himself up on an elbow and listened carefully. He could now faintly hear a brass band, far away, playing a popular marching tune, and on the wind came the sound of church bells. Tom knelt on the bed, lifted his window higher and leaned out. What he first saw and heard was a man firing a shotgun into the air, the report echoing out, and back, like thunder. And the crowd roared its approval. Boys and girls, shouting all the while, ran excitedly after hats thrown into the air and launched them again as soon as they landed. Everyone was dancing. No music was needed, but all cheered when first a fiddle was heard, and they cheered again when an accordion joined in.

"Hey!" Tom shouted down from his third-story window. "Hey!"

A young man heard, looked up. His eyes were bright, his smile wide. He cupped his hand to his ear.

"What's this all about?" The answer came to him even as the words left his mouth.

"The war, Mr. Vincent," the boy shouted up, "it's over!" He looked over his shoulder quickly, then back up at Tom.

Tom waved. The boy turned and joined the dance.

Tom withdrew, closed the window, then sat on the edge of the bed. Long after the celebrants had moved on to Water Street, he was sitting there still.

Very late that night George visited, a copy of *The Evening Mail* tucked beneath his arm. Madeline let him into the room, Tom was sitting in an armchair. Softly closing the door, she left them alone. George held out the newspaper, but Tom shook his head. "Tell me about our boys," he said.

George folded the paper, stuck it beneath his arm again and sat in a chair facing Tom. He searched for the right words.

"Tell me," Tom said.

George coughed, exhaled a long breath. "I'm ... I'm sorry," he said.

Tom nodded. "How many?"

"A few ... only a few made it through." He coughed again. "Here, it's all here." He held out the paper.

In great block letters the headlines

ARMISTICE SIGNED!
WAR WITH GERMANY ENDS!

Tom stared at the words as if they were beyond comprehension. Then he snatched the newspaper from George. "Where is it?" he asked.

George pointed to the bottom right-hand corner.

" 'Cruellest Fate,' " Tom read quietly. " 'While the Empire celebrates, an especially keen sense of loss is being felt throughout Newfoundland. Fifty-eight — ' " He paused, then began again, " 'Fifty-eight of the sixty-seven conscripts who sailed for England just short weeks ago will never again return to the bays and islands from whence they came. Now that the families of the fallen have all been notified, officials in the Office of War Information, who commended the soldiers for their bravery and courageous conduct under fire, were able to confirm that fifty-eight of our native sons succumbed to wounds sustained in actions on the western front on October 29th and 30th. Among the last soldiers to be sent into fray, it was also their fate to be among the last to make the supreme sacrifice. . . .' " He silently read on for a minute more, then dropped the paper beside his chair.

George sighed, then spoke, in a rush, "You should know there's a rumour too, no — more than rumour — it's in the paper there, and Hammond says it's true — that Caines is up for a knighthood. For his part in the war, they say, for the Coalition. For conscription."

Tom shook his head, raised hands and face to the ceiling as if pleading for solace from there.

Looking at George, he said, "Thanks for the paper. You did the right thing."

Then, alone with his thoughts, Tom sat for a long time. He began to cry softly, elbows on his knees, his head hanging. Great teardrops splashed on the floor. Quietly, Madeline entered the room and stood beside him, her hand on his shoulder, on the back of his head.

He wanted whisky then more than at any time in his life. But he knew that if he could go without it, if he could accept and fight through that pain, he would never need it again. He also knew the opposite to be true.

He called to mind that day on Reach Run Island long ago when he'd first squeezed the rich black soil through his hands. He called on the strength he'd felt coursing through him then. He called it to return and run through him again.

One evening he wanted to know what had happened between Wes and herself. It took a long time to tell him fully and honestly of the times Wes had turned on her and struck her and of the many times she'd been betrayed.

Her turn to cry; his to comfort.

The day finally came when he had to sit behind his desk and survey all that was collected there. Work, of all kinds. He touched nothing.

"Tomorrow," he said, "I'll get back at it."

Then he turned and asked if she'd help.

Yes.

To a stack of cancelled cheques, all paid to the order of "Self," all signed by Tom and all written at one time or another on the Collective's business accounts, Madeline added one more.

And no record as to where the money went.

She looked up at Tom from where she was kneeling on the floor. Neat stacks and mounds of all kinds, carefully sorted receipts and bills and correspondence surrounded her. Tom was at his desk working intently. He was planning a trip to Europe. The end of the war made it imperative that, as Minister of Fisheries, he evaluate the stability of the fish markets there.

She took the cheques to him.

"Tom?"

"Yes?"

"I need your help."

"Of course," he said, and motioned for her to sit.

"Look at these for me, please," she said, placing the cancelled cheques before him.

He took one off the top, studied it for a moment, then laid it down. Then he took the lot and riffled them under his thumb. "Expenses," he said quietly. "Miscellaneous."

"Miscellaneous?"

He nodded.

Madeline leaned forward. "Tom," she said, "your 'Miscellaneous' expenses are greater than the cost of running a good many of your union stores. Do you know that?"

He did not answer. "Where'd the money go?" she asked.

"I don't know. Lodgings."

"Sure there's money enough unaccounted for here to *buy* a lodging house."

"Whisky!" he said. Sharply.

He jumped up from his desk then and went to the window, his back to her. "Booze," he said. "Booze. And women. And I don't know. Whatever I wanted. I just lost track, is all. Strayed away."

PART VII

June, 1919.

As the skiff clears the headland, the distinctive slow stroke of the six-horsepower gas motor engine sounds suddenly louder. On the wharf, pitching or splitting fish, loading or unloading the schooners, the men look up from their work. The boat turns into Union Cove and after that a glance now and then is enough to mark its progress until someone says, "There are policemen on board."

As the boat nears the wharf, they are curious to know what this is all about, so they stop what they're doing to watch the arrival of the skiff.

They know the boat by the man at the wheel.

Sitting on the bow thwart, two blue uniforms: they lean shoulder-to-shoulder into the wind, heads down and together, hats hanging in their hands between their knees. They talk, laugh.

The engine cut, the boat glides the last yards to the wharf. The two policemen, smiling, look up. Surprised to have already arrived, they assume dour expressions and pull their shoulders back. They tug their hats on and survey those looking down at them from the wharf.

Lines are thrown, the boat tied up.

On the wharf the policemen nod. The taller of the two is older, grizzled, big and broad; the younger is fair-haired.

"Hello."

"Good day."

"Hello. Hello."

Pleasant enough.

"What can we do for you fellas today?" someone standing near the taller policemen asks. "Don't often see a single constable up this way, let alone two come together."

The tall policeman stands with legs wide apart. His younger partner stands beside him, hands in fists on his hips. They are unarmed. The sun flashes off their big brass buttons, the brass badges on their hats.

"How about a drop o' the 'shine?" the tall one asks, smiling.

The men smile back, shake their heads. "We still under prohibition?"

"That's right."

"And moonshining is still against the law?"

"Right again."

"Well, sir, there's no one in Union Cove would break the law, sir."

Not a soul, is heard in chorus, no one.

"That's not what we hear," the tall constable says.

"Is that right now? Well what are you hearing?"

The younger policeman crosses his arms. "That there's a still on the Island."

"That right? Who'd you hear that from?"

" 'nonymous tip."

Derisive grunts.

"And who does Mister Tip say is keeping a still on the Island?"

They do not answer.

The tall policeman looks up and down the wharf. Loads of lumber, coal and salt in bins, casks of molasses. And fish everywhere: on the wharf dry-hard ready to go. On the angled roofs of the fish store, the cold storage, the cooperage and the fish dryer, damp fish is spread to dry, and the just-caught fish waits to be split and washed, salted and stored.

"No shortage of work here, lads," the tall one says finally. "I heard you Union fellas had the best fit-out premises in the country. Must be good to have everything you need right where you needs it, eh?"

"Oh, yes sir, best kind. There's a salt store in there too."

"There's nothing like this any place else that I know of." The constable paused. "Okay," he says then with a sigh, "now everybody gather round. Good, good. Listen close now fellas. My name's Tucker, and this is Constable Babstock. Why don't one of you give me and Frank the tour and afterwards then you can show me how to get to — what's that fella's name, Frank?"

"Templeman. Isaac Templeman."

"Yah. Isaac Templeman. Do you know where he lives?"

"Oh, for sure."

"Good. Show me after our lookabout, will ya?"

"For sure. Be glad to."

"Good! Now, fellas, do you understand the meaning of what I'm saying? Cause that's all I can say. We're not looking to cause anyone any trouble here today."

Oh, everyone understands well enough. So, as the constables are guided through the premises, as everyone gets back to loading and unloading, pitching and splitting, someone lights out to find Isaac.

After their tour of the premises Constables Tucker and Babstock amble up to Isaac Templeman's house, mustard-coloured, small and square, with a flat sloping roof. A shed, smaller but the same shape and colour, is out back.

Isaac is not at home. Sophie, his wife, has been expecting them, does not know where Isaac is or when he'll be back.

On the wall an engraved wooden plaque reads: TEACH US THY WAY, O LORD.

She swears to God Isaac has never spoken to her of a still. The constables suppose they'll have to look around anyway, but first they accept Mrs. Templeman's offer of tea and raisin buns.

When the tea is drunk and the bun basket empty, the constables can put it off no longer.

After thanking the missus, they go to the shed and as they pull out a folding false wall with accordion-style pleats, they meet Isaac Templeman, in a sweat, on his way in. He is moments too late to save himself.

The constables give him a date, a time and a place to appear before the magistrate.

. . .

This evening the talk is not about the constables. They had their job to do, after all, and were fair enough about it. There'd been plenty of time to break the bloody still down if anyone could've found Isaac or someone else who knew where it was. But Isaac's still was new and known only to Isaac and a few trusted friends, and they'd all been in the woods, taking their time coming home, when someone met Isaac with the news that the constables were looking for him.

But all of that was hashed over before the constables departed the Island. The talk this evening concerns the identity of the informant. If you can't trust your friends, then who in the name of God, Isaac wants to know, can you trust? And he looks at the few men who knew of his handiwork and he doubts not a single one. Who then? He sits, elbows on the table, his left eye looking out between the separated fingers of his right hand. Who, then, could have seen him come and go? Seen what he was carrying into the shed?

"Soph," he rasps. He clears his throat. "Soph!" he says louder. He straightens up, hands on the edge of the table. Sophie is knitting in the rocking chair behind him. He does not turn when he speaks to her. "What did you tell them constables, Sophie?"

"I already told you exactly what I told them." She lets her knitting fall into her lap. "I said that you never said nothing to me about a still and no more you never. But don't you ever think that I didn't know what you were doing. You shouldn't been at it. Now ask me no more questions about it. That's all you're ever going to get from me."

Silence. The click of the knitting needles again.

Isaac grunts, looks into the eyes around the room. "Well, that's that, isn't it?" He adds with a sigh, "Oh, Teach Me Thy Way, O Lord."

GREENSPOND MAGISTRATE'S COURT

Isaac Templeman of Union Cove. First Offence. Guilty of Unauthorized Distillation of Alcohol. Fined: Fifty ($50.00) Dollars. Equipment used in processing to be confiscated, dismantled and destroyed.

. . .

Sir Claude Caines, K.B.E., Prime Minister, and perpetual Justice Minister (Acting), expertly spins the sheet of paper so that it floats through the air and lands in the centre of his desk. He sinks thoughtfully back into his chair, his small hands laced across his small belly.

"And where is Mr. Vincent, our Minister of Fisheries, these days?" he asks no one in particular. "Is he still . . . unwell?"

"In fact, sir," the Prime Minister's secretary, replies, "Mr. Vincent's been back for some time now. But he is, I believe, on his way to Europe. At our request, I might add. To investigate the strength of the codfish markets there, now that the war is over."

"Oh, yes, of course," the Prime Minister says. "I completely forgot about that. You see, as long as he's not in my way, I don't care what he does. The less I have to think about him, the better." He leans forward, crosses his arms on the desk. "Perhaps that's just as well then." He glances at the court report again. "They discovered a still on Our Island, in Union Cove. The very heart of Mr. Vincent's district." His right eye blinks twice, the right corner of his mouth twitches. "I believe there's more than one there."

"But, sir —" Anthony tries to interject.

"*I think*," Caines loudly overrules, "that we need to search for more . . . for more of these illegal distilleries, to search for them, to seize and destroy them. Send in more men, Anthony. Don't use the local constables. Send our own city men. They're tougher, they have more experience with moonshiners. They'll know what to do."

2

On the uppermost deck of the *CLIO*, just to see if he could remember, Tom taps out the Morse code. And then the international code. Funny he couldn't simply recite the codes out of his head. No. He had to sit at a table and set his arm as if he were at the key, and use a pen to tap, so the ear would have something to hear, and only then did the signals come down clear and easy through the years, the many years since he'd practised telegraphy.

A — *dit-dah*; B — *dah-dit-dit-dit*; C — *dah-dit-dah-dit*, and so on.

He considers the importance of taking the right posture, of assuming the proper attitude, to call up the past.

He is the only person on the deck and the North Atlantic air is fresh, not cold, but cold enough to keep most of the other passengers inside, which suits him perfectly.

The door behind him opens, closes softly. Without a word or even a glance in Tom's direction, Hammond strolls to the rail. He looks out, snaps up the collar of his raglan, then turns his back on the great Atlantic to face Tom.

They are both smiling.

Tom motions with his hand to an empty chair, an invitation Hammond accepts. He sits at the edge of the chair and leans forward with hands in his pockets, looking as if, rather than arriving, he were readying to stand and leave.

"Why, Mr. Janes," Tom says, smiling still, "what a coincidence. Tell me, your trip is for pleasure, or business?"

"Both," a now unsmiling Hammond says matter-of-factly. "*The Mail* decided to pay half-fare after I convinced them this would be a singular opportunity for me to talk to you."

Tom nods. "I see." Then he is serious and silent for a time, watching the sea.

Gray weather erasing the horizon.

Tom, still looking away, says, "I was thinking just now of telegraphy. I can tell you about those times, start there if you want, or earlier than that if you like." He turns his head to Hammond. "If you're interested in all that."

"I'm interested." And now Hammond dares to lean back in his chair. "The beginning," he says. "That and the conscription vote."

"Hmm," Tom says.

Hammond shrugs. "That's the part *The Mail* really wants, what they're paying for."

It is clear in Tom's glance away that he reconsiders momentarily, but then he says, "Well, that's only fair, I suppose. As you say, the moment is opportune. We're out of Newfoundland's troubled waters. Will be for some time. So, while I am feeling free, Hammond, let's do it once and for all."

Now it is dark on deck, except for the weak yellow light shining through the door window, and even though it is June, the North Atlantic night is chill.

Sometime during their talk Madeline has quietly joined them, her hair long and loose, and Tom fit her close and comfortable and warm to his side.

Never before has Hammond seen them so, they have never been as relaxed with him. Hammond has never felt as close to this centre, so he does not interrupt. He does not want this to end.

But it does, testily.

"C'mon Hammond, for God's sake, let's go eat. We can carry on with this tomorrow, you know, and the day after that, too, if you want. Plenty o' time."

"Okay. Tomorrow."

3

Four constables tie up their own boat at the wharf in Union Cove. This time the fishermen are puzzled and uneasy. Twice within the month is hard to fathom. And these officers are not like the first two, for sure. They don't ask directions or request a walkabout. You just step back and make room for these four when they march your way, glaring at you.

Straight into town they march. In pairs and without warning they enter and search the first two houses on the road, come out empty-handed. Everyone stops work to wait and see what next they will do. Some of the men hurry into their homes as soon as the constables come out, to calm the nerves of those inside, women and children and old men mainly. The constables had nothing to say but were in a black mood, more unspoken threat than real menace to person or property, as if they were doing it all for show.

The constables boldly enter the next two homes along, and as before, find nothing. They are about to move on but notice the fishermen have grown in number and are staying close behind them.

Now and then glancing over their shoulders, the constables confer in the middle of the road, and change their minds it seems, because suddenly they turn and stride back towards the fishermen. They look neither right nor left. The fishermen let them pass, but at the wharf more fishermen are waiting: more than a dozen, their eyes hard and bright and steady. They are in an ugly mood and block the way to the boat. It is clear to the constables that it would be of no use to order or even ask the fishermen to stand aside. There is no choice but to climb down the wharf, then slowly shuffle all the long way across its face to get to their boat.

They start their engine right away, cast off, then turn to head out of the cove. Before they get up speed, three boats loaded with men come out of nowhere to intercept them. The constables have to cut their engine.

The boats move closer, hook onto the captive boat with gaffs, then cut their engines. Except for the sound of someone wetly coughing, there is a heavy, pressing silence.

The constables sit, their nervousness showing in stillness. The fishermen are standing comfortably, staring steadily, some unable to hide grins. Every now and then one of the constables catches a fisherman's eye that wickedly winks. All are quiet, dangerously quiet, so as to unnerve the constables. Finally:

"What are you doing in Union Cove?"

Orders. Stills. Search and destroy. That's all the constables know, or so they say.

Using the gaffs, the fishermen start to rock the policemen's boat. They start slowly, but after a few strong pushes and pulls, the gunnels touch water, the boat stands on alternate sides. The constables, screaming and shouting, holding onto their hats, scramble up one side of the boat and then the other to keep it from capsizing. Suddenly they are let go, set adrift, terrified and diminished.

"Don't come back!" someone calls.

"But if you do," shouts another, "mind your manners!"

And there is laughter in all the fishermen's boats.

But the constables do not hear it. They are intent only on speeding out of the cove.

One of their hats, riding the wake of their boat, fills slowly with water, burbles, then goes under, the device showing up brightly once as the hat turns and sinks out of sight.

Caines sighs. Why did he ever think that going up against Tom Vincent, even when he was out of the country, would be easy?

"Send the constables back with more men. Arrest the men that kept them from doing their duty." He thinks a moment. "One more thing. Arm the constables this time, please."

4

Two days later the four constables are back in Union Cove with fifteen of their mates and a gray-haired sergeant, and the sergeant is the only one not carrying a rifle.

The fishermen see them coming, watch them form up on the wharf. This gives them time to prepare.

But the first resistance the policemen meet this day is Mother May, who, as she is wont to do of late, is out walking the road, talking to familiar spirits, and it happens that she simply wanders into the policemen. When she sees their guns, she cannot control herself. *"How dare you venture down here with your danger!"* she shouts at them. She is small, pale and frail and in a black mourning dress and she charges ineffectually into the four-abreast formation, swinging wildly at the policemen. *"Away from this island with those guns,"* she screams. *"Wasn't the war enough of guns?"*

The column comes to a halt, stands at attention.

Another woman is suddenly there to step in and take Mother May by the wrist, to lay an arm across her shoulders. She pulls her close, soothes words into her ear and leads her quietly away.

Further on, the armed force finds a contingent of fishermen blocking their way. The fishermen are as well-armed as the police, but hold their rifles loosely at the ready, and they outnumber the police two to one. They have men enough to both face and flank.

Everything stops. The only sound is Hedley Waye's wet cough.

The surprised sergeant tries to speak, but stammers, and then his voice is lost in the fishermen's hooting and shouting, in their threats and angry taunting. The policemen, paling, stand silent, jaws clamped together. A nervous young one of them unshoulders his rifle, and in blurry motion, as if in some benign rifle drill that all present have long practised together, all weapons are unshouldered or raised, cocked or bolted into firing position, both sides achieving aim at the same moment.

Then all is silent again. Standoff.

The sergeant slowly raises his right hand, a signal to all to hold fire. Hand still in the air, he cautiously turns to face his men. In a steady voice, he gives the order to shoulder arms. No one moves. He repeats his order, louder than before, but still the policemen do not move. He waits another moment for compliance, then he abandons his official posture, speaks to them in a normal tone of voice. "Fellas," he says, "do as I say." Surprised by his change of voice, some of the policemen look at him now. He nods to affirm that what he is ordering, what he is saying, is what they must do. Gradually then, the policemen relax, lower their weapons, stand at ease. The sergeant lowers his hand, looks back over his shoulder, and the fishermen lower their weapons, too. The sergeant nods his approval and turns back to his own men. He orders an about-face, and with the fishermen keeping pace behind them, they march quickstep back to their boats.

When he hears that even this larger force of policemen have been shamefully driven from the cove, Caines is dumbstruck that these fishermen, mere fishermen, are so openly and so boldly challenging the authorities, *his* authority in particular.

It is perhaps time, he thinks, to teach the island renegades something about the exercise of power.

He closes his office door, slouches in his chair.

5

All the young fishermen of Union Cove, all but Hedley Waye, have gone North to pursue the Labrador fishery.

Hedley's cough had come on a cold that slowly thickened in his head and then his lungs. He had taken to bed, and in bed he's been now for three days and three nights. He does not eat and as time passes and the illness blocks in thicker still, he pales and sleeps long and deep, but not restfully or curatively.

Those watching over him fear he is nearing death.

Before the dawning of the fourth day of July, a British battleship, the HMS *Kent*, slides quietly through the dark waters off Our Island. The *Kent* cuts speed and for a time patrols slowly back and forth across the mouth of Union Cove, as if keeping watch over the sleeping port. Then the ship takes a position, and spotting icebergs white in the night and some distance away, it commences gunnery practice.

The first volley rends the dark with a rip of light, thunders the quiet down, breaking sleep.

Mother May startles awake. Without a thought she swings out of bed, too quickly for aging bones, and all at once she feels pain all over. Her hands reach up and out in the dark, searching for anything to hold on to, anything to balance her, but she falls to the floor, saved from breaking bones only by the bedclothes that partially hold her as in a sling. Head near the floor, legs trapped, she hangs, disoriented.

The thunder thumps again, the windowpanes rattle, the water jug trembles in its basin.

Mother May elbows herself out of the tangle of bedclothes. She stands, one hand to her head, the other groping the dark. She finds the night table. She knows, even in the dark, exactly where the framed picture of her slain soldier-son stands on that table. She knows always where she is in relation to it.

She takes the picture to her bosom, and with her other hand pulls out the night table drawer. She draws her son's pistol from its holster.

Making small frightened cries, she scurries to the window. She pulls at the curtain, awkwardly and too hard, so curtain and curtain rod come down, startling her again. She steps back, as it falls at her feet. She stares through the window, squinting, searching the dark.

Everything flashes intensely white, thunder punches her stomach.

In the lightning moment, the battleship stands out huge and mighty, a bas-relief of light and shadow, of menacing metal projections, the devil surfaced in the mind of Mother May, come at last in demon machinery.

She stares blankly and waits, one hand holding the picture of her son, and the other his revolver.

She waits. For him. To appear.

The bombardment of the icebergs wakes Hedley Waye. His wife is looking out the window. He thinks he speaks to her. My Jesus, he thinks he says, what size bullets are they using? I have to see. Then he is walking down to the slipway, and he hears his wife call to him, and he is about to turn when the sky whitens, blinding him for a moment. There in the light, marching, a column of policemen and soldiers, rifles ready, but Hedley is prepared to fight. He turns to rally his brothers-in-arms but all there is is his wife's voice screeching through the darkness.

Is it raining? he wonders. What is happening? And he faints.

By mid-morning the policemen and the soldiers have searched every house and scoured the Island. Everyone tells them the same thing. They're on the coast of Labrador.

Hedley Waye has been arrested.

He is in some kind of delirium, a poor prize considering all the work the soldiers and policemen have done, but better than no prize at all, so over the wailing of his wife and the tears and protests of all those left on the Island, they take him away.

Mother May sees it all. Sees how all will be taken by armies out of the dark.

She is ready. They enter her house. She hears them downstairs: heavy boots, doors opening and closing. She hears the boots on the stairs. She turns slowly from the window, and when she hears the soldier at her door, she points her son's gun and waits.

"I'm not ready," she says calmly.

"I must check all rooms, ma'am," comes the reply.

"I'm hardly dressed," she says, "but, for Heaven's sake, do as you must."

Keeping the pistol aimed at the door she moves to her bed. She drops her son's picture softly there, then pulls the hammer back with her thumbs, surprised it clicks back so easily.

Outside the door the soldier says, "Never mind, ma'am."

Mother May carefully lays the gun on the night table.

That afternoon the battleship is authorized to intercept any and all boats necessary in order to identify and arrest all the fishermen involved in the recent rioting on the Island.

So the *Kent* weighs anchor, and sets its course for the coast of Labrador.

Hedley Waye, prisoner, on board.

Tom was surprised how close the battlefields were to Paris. Once out of the city it was smooth driving, and then a long slow curve into low rolling hills, and then they were there.

Once he turned to make sure Madeline and Hammond were with him. He fully opened the ground of imagination and just like that heard guns and screaming. *What the hell!* he thought, suddenly echoing. The sky deep blue, but as he looked up it shaded darker as if smoke, the floating debris of war, were yet contaminating the air. And the earth itself felt uncertain beneath his feet, soft and damp here, hard and metallic there, and all of unpredictable contour. He felt vague anxieties, and his hearing was particularly acute, alert to every sound, the sound of his feet scraping earth, a scratch across eardrums. Something terrible about to happen. So he stopped, and suddenly he saw himself standing there, the only thing standing. For miles and miles, everything was flat, scarred, even the earth hurt, pulverized, and he crouched down, held his farmer's hands over the earth, as if to warm them over a fire and indeed he felt a heat radiate from the earth, as one feels heat rise from a tenderness on the body, and he closed his eyes: images of the boys he had called and sent, boys who died the terrible deaths and through his head, as if through his eyes, roared a flood of visions of incredible death, bodies opened, separated and spilling, and life lifting in escape from the mess of murder. Tom stood, opened his eyes, hands still in front of him, shaking now and sweating, and tears, and tears, and he turned to look back, making sure Madeline and Hammond were still there.

Smell of smoke in the air.

7

*F*or weeks now Tom and Madeline and Hammond had taken most of their meals together, Hammond still waiting for answers. Now, so as to soften the shock of their return to St. John's, the first day back from Europe, they breakfast together at Tom's, and afterwards take the long leisurely stroll to the Colonial Building.

Just inside the doors, they encounter Caines hurrying along. "Sorry about your trouble, Tom," he says without slackening his pace.

Tom stops. "And what might that be?" he asks of Caines' back, but Caines scurries on.

After a moment Tom turns and, muttering a curse underneath his breath, strides quickly the other way, Madeline and Hammond following. Tom stops the next person they meet and asks, "Have you seen George Gill?"

It is well after midnight and the inner circle of the FC has its sleeves rolled. Madeline is curled in a chair, her mind hazed and her eyes red and tired. Hammond is there also, a trusted confidant.

Hammond and Madeline and the others have watched Tom pace back and forth behind his desk as he heard argument and counter-argument, time and time, and time again.

"I'm going to take the yacht and go after them," he says finally. "Look," he says patiently, "the fishermen feel I betrayed them on conscription ... and perhaps they are right. This is my chance to redeem myself — it's as simple as that. The way I see it I have no choice. I must do this." Looking at those who shake their heads, those whose arguments have failed to dissuade him, he continues. "If we're lucky, we'll get to them before the Brits. We know they'll fish

Punch Bowl. The Brits don't know that. They don't even know where to start looking. If we leave right away, I think we'll get there before the Brits find them. We'll cover the *FC*'s name. Madeline will come with me. She and I will be a couple on a recreational excursion if anyone asks. Hammond can be our guest, if he wants." Tom looks at him, Hammond nods. Tom smiles. "Good," he says. "Now, George, you go up to the cove and do whatever needs to be done. The rest of you can stay here, do what you can with the newspapers. Drive it home that these fishermen are running away from *nothing*, that they're doing as they do this time every year."

The circle nods and mumbles in acquiescence, then someone asks, "What will you do when you get there, Tom? I mean if they've taken some of them, or all of them?"

Tom shrugs. "I don't know. We'll see. They already have Hedley Waye. Whether they have one or a dozen, it's still the same problem, isn't it? Anyway we'll see."

As soon as they are out of St. John's harbour, they set the *FC* on a course for the Funk Islands, and are lucky enough to catch a fair wind. Smooth sailing all that day and night. Next morning, the Funks on the horizon, they set the course for Cape Bauld, the wind keeping the sails filled. On the third morning out, they cross the Strait of Belle Isle. Fitful winds, turbulent water, slow progress, but on the other side, gentler waters and a steady breeze. Midafternoon, they chance upon most of their schooners anchored within sight of one another, not further north in the Punch Bowl after all, but off Berry Bight.

In no time at all, the purpose of their visit has travelled from schooner to schooner. Men are called from the water, summoned from labours on deck or below. Soon, from every schooner, skiffs set out and converge on the *FC*.

Carrying suitcases and boxes and white calico clothes bags, the fishermen from Union Cove climb aboard the *FC* looking sad and serious, unsure.

Tom is there to welcome them. He smiles, shakes each man's hand, sends them below where hot meals are waiting.

8

"Wake up! Wake up!" a voice orders, and Captain Emmet Torraville, of the *W. Johnston*, feels a stiff poke in the back. Instantly he is alert.

Something is happening, he thinks, just as Tom said it would.

"I'm awake," Emmet says softly.

He blinks, then slowly turns from the wall to see three of them standing there, but it is the muzzle of the rifle that gave him the poke, that points at him still, that rules the cramped cabin space. Emmet winces. Two uniformed sailors, one young, one old, the young one with a stripe holding the rifle. A uniformed policeman leans close to see Emmet the better. Emmet glimpses the first mate standing helplessly behind them. Emmet comes to sitting. He raises a hand in front of the muzzle, looks down and away. The policeman studies him carefully, then shakes his head.

"No," says the policeman, "he's not one of them."

Some tension in the air dissolves.

The rifle is lowered and the safety locked on. Both the sailors and the policemen take a step back and Emmet lets out a long relieved breath.

"My, oh my," he says, shaking his head. "My, oh my, oh my."

"Do you know any of these fishermen?" the stripe asks, pressing on regardless in a thick English accent. Rifle hanging from the crook of his arm, the sailor reads the names from a sheet of paper. Emmet nods 'Yes' to every one.

"I know them all," Emmet says when the list is finished.

"Where are they now?" the older sailor asks, his voice soft and deep.

Emmet shakes his head.

"Did any of these men ship with you?" the stripe demands. Emmet nods, tells him the names.

"Where are they now?" the old sailor asks again.

Emmet is silent.

Then the policeman says, "These men are wanted men, you know. Wanted for disturbing the peace."

"How many have you found so far?" Emmet asks, interrupting.

"Can't tell you that," the young sailor snaps.

But later, when they are leaving Emmet's schooner empty-handed, the old sailor hangs back a moment, whispers in Emmet's ear. "We've only one," he says, "and we took him off the island. Your man Vincent is getting to them all before us, and we don't know him or his boat."

Swift and smooth, the heavy engine powered the *FC* through the night, and dangerously too, some might say, for the three-masted schooner showed no lights at all. But with the night sky star-thick and radiant, and a good part of the moon patterning the gentle dark sea, there was light enough.

And while Tom and Madeline and Hammond were out all evening talking and laughing on the foredeck, the outlaw fishermen took turns coming up from below, singly or in pairs, to stretch and to smoke.

As it was night and no other boats were to be seen, Tom mocked the fishermen's caution in a friendly fashion and urged the lot of them to come up, but he convinced them neither to show themselves all at once nor to lengthen their time above decks. So Tom ordered all hatches and doors and portholes open. "In cramped quarters they may be," said Tom, "but they will at least breathe the good free air."

For some time now, however, none had come up to make a round, and raucous snoring was sometimes sounding out even to the foredeck.

It was very late.

Madeline, cocooned in a heavy blanket, had fallen asleep curled up on one of the deck chairs.

Hammond thinking this was so familiar they could be on the *CLIO* still, their visit to the field of battle yet to come, or they could be on the return trip, this present trouble undreamt of. Because, he thought, all these voyages were very much alike, and that notion unfixed time for him somehow. There was Tom in dark silhouette, head and shoulders against the starground and it was for the moment as if they had entered a different realm altogether wherein some hitherto hidden truth might be revealed. And then it was, when all things of the day gone by had fallen away, and the day to come was yet without form, that Tom began to speak, soft and low:

"I was separate from my earth so long, I had no strength left to oppose the world.

"I just got tired, you know.

"The moment we were the balance of power, all the decisions we had to make and all the votes we had to cast, they were all important, and we were all new to government . . . "

How suddenly events and attendant troubles sometimes reverse:

That night the battleship makes a great wide turn, then runs south, on a course parallel to Tom's.

At first light, the *FC* has to come to a full stop, for a high gray wall of steel blocks the way.

Tom stands on deck with Madeline. Everyone else is below, in hiding. He looks about in the early morning light. There is a stiff breeze.

On a sign from Tom, the *FC* inches forward. Tom takes a position on the bow, hands on the rails, leaning slightly forward, one foot slightly back, just to brace himself.

Guns, everyone is thinking, they're turning guns on us now.

The little *FC* slaps closer and closer and when Tom judges they are close enough, he raises his hand and the engine is cut. Then Tom and Madeline crane their necks, searching for some sign, and then a pair of hands take hold of the rails high above, then a hat full of gold braid appears, and shouts down: "Ahoy, cruiser! Medical emergency!

We've bit of a medical emergency on our hands. Passenger. Done what we can for him. Still very sick. Needs more than we have here, I'm afraid, but we're on duty . . . we're hoping you can run him back for us?"

"Aye, aye!" Tom shouts back. "We can take care of him."

And Hedley Waye is delivered back into the hands of his own people.

Aboard the *FC*, there is no time to celebrate. Full speed south.

But Tom orders a course as close to the coast as the helmsman dares and stands on deck watching the land, looking for what he does not know. But he has felt something move inside him again. He will know what he needs when he sees it.

He closes his eyes, looks inward and sees Hedley Waye, so thin and pale, breath so shallow, wet and thick with infection.

They'd wrapped him in blankets. Tom asked Madeline to watch over him, ordered the cook to boil water so it would be ready the instant it was needed.

And the granite land slips by, slides from cliff to brown barrens tufted with trees and Tom signals for his boat to slow, to move closer to the land.

Twenty minutes later, Tom and three of his men step ashore.

Tom is intense, inspired. He steps this way, that way, an animal sniffing a trail. He spies a bush, walks to it, hauls the bush up but not completely out of the earth. He scrapes at the moss around the bush, pulls at the plant again until its tangle of thin roots are loose and exposed.

"Take these," he orders, "wash them in sea water, put them in the dory. Keep them covered."

While the others do as ordered, Tom strides over to one of the thin trees and with a fingernail makes a small slit in the rind, which he splits, then strips from the trunk.

They are not long back on the *FC* before the air fills with odours that stick sharp and high in the nose, bring tears to the eyes, and drive all except those who must be on hand above decks.

The boiled bark is thick and pulpy. Tom carefully separates the fibrous strings from the mash which he spoons into a bowl and lets stand and cool for several minutes. Then he gives the bowl to Madeline, who slowly dribbles the broth into Hedley Waye's mouth.

Tom watches for results, continues in the meantime to instruct the others how to strain the essence out of the roots.

The boilers still boiling. The air humid. Everyone sweats.

Hedley Waye, quite suddenly, not so much coughs as convulses, and that motion repeats, again and again, until his eyes are wide open, frightened. Deep down, a black plug of disease is loosened, dislodged, spat out. Hedley is on the edge of his berth now, gasping for breath still, his breath wheezing and congested, but now there is the rattle of an open airway. Weak and shaking, sweating, his eyes confused, defeated. So Tom sits beside him, puts his arm across Hedley's shoulder. Madeline does likewise on the other side.

Tom orders blankets to be draped over all three of them together and pots of steaming hot water placed before them, so the steam can rise into Hedley's face, rise into his nostrils and lungs to saturate and loosen the clotted congestion. Tom calls now for the bush root, tastes it, spits it out. He is about to hand it back, but Hedley rests his hand on Tom's. He wants it just as it is. He drinks. He coughs and spits. Coughs and spits and coughs and spits until his lungs are scoured. And when at last they lay him back in his berth, he is asleep before his head touches the pillow. His breathing is clear, deep and even. Everything and everyone below decks is slick and wet and warm.

After Hedley is wrapped comfortably in his berth, Tom opens the hatch. Sweet cool air of morning and sounds of sea birds come in with the light.

The morning air makes him shiver, and he is shivering still when he gives the order to set a course for Union Cove.

9

Tom and Madeline are alone on deck when Union Cove rises out of the horizon. They'd been walking slowly, talking low, laughing, happy to be together, he with his hands in his pockets and staring down at the deck, she holding his arm.

"Good," Tom says. "Good to see it again at last."

"Yes."

Quiet a long time, the two of them, watching the island grow larger.

"What are you thinking?"

"It's good," Tom says again. "Good to see it."

He is bringing the fishermen safely home to Union Cove, to the place, the action he'd birthed out of thin air.

And the cove crowded with coastal schooners. *Austin and Paul*, *KJH*, *Carmelita* and *Edward K.*: He knows them all by cut of sail.

When the *FC* ties up at the wharf, flags are flying and signs of welcome are everywhere. Everyone has come out to greet them and George is waiting, having orchestrated it all.

All hands are on deck, smiling, and the crowd claps and stomps and cheers and those on board wave to those on the wharf.

Tom and Madeline walk down the gangplank. As soon as they step off the crowd pushes close, wanting to shake their hands or slap them on the back, just to touch them, and, strangely, in all the commotion, a thin white hand calmly holds out a framed picture. Such an odd offering that, after a moment, Tom takes the picture, turns it right side up, tries to make sense of it as he is jostled about.

Head and shoulders: a young soldier, a scarred chin.

Tom feels the comfortable press of the crowd, hears a cheer go up for the fishermen he rescued, just now stepping off the *FC*.

The picture still in his hand is a puzzle, and he is distracted by it. He wants to give it back. He sees the thin hand reach and he returns the picture to it. He follows the hand as it pulls the picture to a frail chest. The woman's hair, all but for one strand, is perfectly kempt. As one white hand carries the picture to protection, the other rises, shaking, a tiny hand barely able to lift the handgun, shaking with the effort of pulling the trigger, and the gun rises to his face. He knocks the hand down, but the gun fires, a loud noise but just a lick of fire, a small hole in Tom's vest, over the heart. His face a sudden mask of pain and surprise.

Everything stops.

For a certain radius around Tom and Madeline, there is a sharp intake of breath, but the rest of the crowd continues to celebrate.

Now Tom falls back in Madeline's arms, blood oozing from the wound. He gasps for a breath, his legs fail.

The woman is easily overcome, the gun seized.

Tom on the wharf, and now there are screams.

Madeline, eyes wide, speechless, kneeling, his head in the crook of her arm. Tom lifts his hand from the wound, looks in wonder at the blood, then at Madeline. Then at George and Hammond Janes. He wants to speak, there is something he wants to say, but he can't.

They look where he looks, see what he sees: In silhouette, the crowd around him. The blue sky, washing to white, and someone nearby holding an FC flag that snaps lively in the wind.

From somewhere it catches the light.

10

Thinking the salon empty and believing this might be his only chance, the mortician orders his assistants to take the body to the front window for display. But Madeline, having spent the solitary night in a state of wakeful fatigue, has just stepped outside at the first bleak light to take the air, to empty herself of the notion of sleep for good.

When she enters the room and sees the assistants about to wheel the body away, she screams, commands them to stop, demands to know on whose orders they are acting. The Director, hearing the commotion, steps out of his office and orders his assistants away, apologizes for their mistake. Madeline is near hysterical, not making much sense at all, speaking out of fatigue and grief. The Director has seen it all before. With quiet words, with a firm and gentle arm across her shoulders, he smoothly soothes her back to her chair by the window, quiet and calm restored.

She looks at Tom no more.

There is a single high and narrow window in the salon. The folds and falls of the window's white curtains translate the light raying through into an intense, diffuse white, a pure white, as if the curtains themselves were the source of light.

Near this window Madeline sits. Across from her, in steady candlelight, lies the body. The FC flag draped over the casket.

On the same ship that carried Mother May to the Asylum in St. John's, Madeline had travelled with Tom. She knows the face of his death better than anyone. She has no need to look at him.

. . .

When Tom was first laid out, she kissed his cold forehead, once and for all.

This morning George, no surprise, is the first to arrive. Weighted down by his overcoat, he greets Madeline with a sad smile, speaks quietly to her. She wants nothing, does not wish to leave, so George nods, takes his place at the foot of the casket.

Madeline watches him as he sits, as he sinks into a well of paralysing grief.

There are constables at the doors when it is time for the general public to be admitted.

The people come in steady numbers throughout the day, each glimpsing the body for only a few moments.

The FC Executive arrives in a buzz of confusion, settles down to pay respects. They all speak to Madeline, then to George, laying hands on his shoulders. Some sit next to him and whisper in his ear, while others, more insistent, plead with him in low and earnest voices. But George cannot be engaged.

Knowing looks are exchanged

They gather in the antechamber. By invitation Madeline joins them.

The talk is all about Caines' treachery in the House. He has killed the FC motion to have a national day of mourning declared.

The FC had tried to mount a challenge but their efforts were weak and disorganized. They hadn't expected resistance, and they are all in shock. Bitter, too, and a little abashed at being so easily outmaneuvered.

Everyone it seems is trying to do things their own way, and nothing is working. They are waiting for George to step forward, to take control, but they know the depth of his grief. He has no heart for any politics now.

Madeline says, "I'll talk to him."

"It's more than grief," George tells her when they are alone. He looks into her eyes, then turns to look out on the harbour. He watches the people and boats, the business as usual.

"I understand," Madeline says.

George bows his head, nods. "Ah, well," he says, "what's happened has happened."

He turns, looks up, motions to a chair, and Madeline sits. He sits across from her.

"While he was alive I tried in every way to be the good lieutenant. I did everything that had to be done, and I came to know the things that had to be done, and I did them for him, before he asked because . . . because everything I was, I became because of him. But I'm no leader. I was a good lieutenant, but I can't lead. I have no head for it. There were some things even he was too late to change."

Madeline says, "But one more time, George, you must be a good lieutenant. One more time."

George sighs. Nods.

Within the hour he calls a meeting.

"I know," George says, "it is what Tom would want us do if he were here."

The response is quiet, respectful, exasperated. "If Tom were here, George, it would not be necessary to do anything."

George stands with his back to the speaker, to the whole FC Executive.

They are meeting in a bare, unused room on the second floor of the funeral salon. White walls and ceiling, polished hardwood flooring, a single window. No furniture but the chairs they have nipped from here and there throughout the building. George's chair the only one not, at this moment, in use.

He stands looking out of the window into the leaves and branches of a maple. He recognizes the voice of the man who just spoke, but it makes no difference. They are all speaking with one voice, against him.

George has been speaking quietly and respectfully — showing them his back is no sign of rancour, but of unwillingness to be fully engaged.

He has suggested that Madeline would be the best person to take over the Presidency of the FC, at least on an interim basis.

The idea had come to him quickasthat as he climbed the stairs to the second floor, and in such clarity and completeness that he did not doubt its rightness at all.

He reminded the dumbstruck Executive that Madeline had recently assisted Tom in putting his offices and all his business affairs in order, so she needed no grounding there. As well, she had travelled to Europe with Tom, so she knew firsthand how matters stood in those countries.

By then the Executive had found its collective voice, and responded that it was wrong all along for Tom to have taken up with the Woolfrey woman the way he had. Best now for the FC if Madeline fell out of public view, for her association with Tom to be quickly forgotten.

For other members the question of Madeline's relationship with Tom and the FC, past or future, did not merit serious discussion. There was no precedent for female leadership, neither in unions nor political parties. It could not happen, certainly not if they wished to hold and increase their power. *That*, they said, is what Tom would truly understand if he were in the room.

George believed his idea had been a true inspiration, but as soon as he made the suggestion, he knew he was trying too hard to be like Tom. The thought also crossed his mind that it could be a long and joyous fight to put Madeline into the Presidency, but he wondered whether or not he possessed the necessary energy and will.

He turns, sits down. There are about a dozen of them, seated without rhyme or reason about the room, their dark mourning suits in stark contrast to the white walls.

"It might be a noble thing to pursue one day, George, but now is not the time." There is a general murmur of support for the speaker. "Right now we need someone all can rally around, in our time of sorrow, you see. We need someone well-known and generally acceptable to all, someone who was close to Tom" — and then there is in the voice, George notes, an unwitting moment of hesitation, meaningful and menacing — "for now." The voice continues, "We have no time for controversy, George. We need you, now. We have arrangements to make. And everything must be as right as rain."

"Why is it, then," George asks, "that the business of government carries on as usual? They are not even flying their flags at half-mast." A thin current of anger is finding its way into his voice. "How did that happen?"

No one answers, no one moves.

"Yes?" George says.

"We ... we weren't expecting opposition." Then, after a moment, "A mistake. Claude Caines..." The thought is left unfinished.

Oh yes, George thinks, there will be some scores to settle. Some right away — with the Prime Minister. Scuttle the ship of state. If I cannot deliver Tom's vision, well then, my own rough version will have to do.

The anger rising in him, hurt and indignant, the pain brought back to him. But he knew how to put that anger into a crowd if he wanted to. He'd seen Tom in high dudgeon torch a church and together they'd strangled the trade of the whole country through blockade. And Tom had sent men off to fight, knowing many of them would die.

After such history, what was it he could not now do?

Late in the evening, Madeline is lightly sleeping, slumped in the chair, the only one left. Lamps are being extinguished, there is the sound of doors being locked and checked. George stands in the doorway to the salon.

"Madeline," he says.

She looks up startled.

"Go home, Madeline. You need sleep. There's no more you can do here. You've done more than your share anyway."

Madeline looks at the coffin. She looks down, then back at George, and nods. "Not right away, though. Come sit with me a few minutes." She pats the seat of the chair next to her. George hesitates a moment, then enters the salon, shuts the door quietly. There is only candlelight, a very private place now. The three of them alone. George sits, looks at Madeline intently. She catches his eye, looks back.

"So," she asks, "how was the meeting?"

George shrugs.

"What's been decided?" she asks.

After a long moment he says, "I'll do what I can."

"You'll do fine," Madeline says, not surprised.

George chuckles. "I don't know," he says. "I hope so." He looks at the casket, then back at Madeline. "He taught us to know our strengths, but he showed us our weaknesses, too. I've no head for it Madeline, or I've the wrong kind of head."

After the service for the Burial of the Dead, the flag-draped casket is closed, then placed on a carriage and drawn through the streets by a team of four horses. Madeline and George follow in a hansom cab, a procession of mourners behind them.

Under clear skies and a bright sun, quiet crowds. Hats come off as the procession slowly winds its way down to Water Street.

Because no day of mourning has been proclaimed, it is business as usual, and on Water Street the workers have worked quietly all morning, eyes to the windows. The moment the procession turns onto Water Street, the workers abandon their machines, leave their loading and unloading, their actions and transactions, checks and re-checks — whatever they are doing, and step quietly out into the streets. In minutes, the business of Water Street is stopped and stilled. The owners take off their glasses, lay down their pens, knowing they cannot keep these people from paying respects.

FC colours, white on the blue ground, are everywhere, and men in union guernseys, despite the heat, line the sides of the street. The sun graces them all. The only sound is the slow tramp of the horses.

There is a longing in the silence that one of the guernseyed men suddenly breaks, shouting, "*Vincent! Tom! President!*" Another man answers, "*Here!*"

Thus begins a call and response that is quickly taken up and down the street, from all quarters of the crowd.

In her cab, as if call and response awaken her, Madeline lifts her head, then the dark thin veil that has shielded her face all morning.

The warm sun on her face, the brightness of the day, the vividness of the FC colours.

They are moving past a barrel-chested man. His voice, above all others, booms out, *"Vincent! Tom! President!"*

Without thinking, she answers.

"Here!"

Acknowledgements

During the writing of *A Settlement of Memory*, I most often consulted the following books: Sir William F. Coaker's *Past, Present and Future: Being a Series of Articles Contributed to the Fishermen's Advocate, 1932*; *A Coaker Anthology*, compiled and edited by Robert H. Cuff; *To Each His Own* by Ian MacDonald; and *The Islands of Bonavista Bay* by John Feltham.

My parents, Chesley and Nellie Rodgers, were living resources and supplied vital information ranging from the nature of women's undergarments (*circa* 1918), to setting a course from St. John's to the coast of Labrador. Time and again, it was my pleasure to call upon them.

Thanks to all those at Killick Press: to Don Morgan and Heather Tucker for patience and continuing interest in my work; to Anne Hart and Bernice Morgan, not only for specific suggestions, but for their belief in the story and trust in the writer; to Ed Kavanagh, a friend who also proved to be an insightful critic and creative motivator; and to Carmelita McGrath who kept the story true to itself in matters both large and small. *A Settlement of Memory* is a better novel because of the involvement of these people.

I consider myself lucky to have met Stan Dragland when this project was nearing completion. He generously agreed to read the novel, and through his painstaking attention to detail brought greater clarity to much of the writing. I am especially grateful to him for his contribution.

I thank Jane Urquhart, who, as Writer-in-Residence at Memorial University of Newfoundland, encouraged me to finish this novel. Her comments on early versions of three short sections were most helpful.

Thank you Paul Bowdring, Kenneth J. Harvey, and Wayne Johnston for interest, inspiration, advice, conversation and friendship over the years.

When the Thursday Writing Group was up and running, the enthusiasm expressed there for this story was important to me.

For various kindnesses shown to me along the way, thank you Karen Crotty, Mary Dalton, Rick Daw, Bert Riggs, and Greg Taaffe.